Always and Forever

Always and Forever

JAMES PRINCE

Order this book online at www.trafford.com
or email orders@trafford.com

Most Trafford titles are also available at major online book retailers.

This is a work of fiction. All of the characters, names, incidents, organizations, and dialogue in this novel are either the products of the author's imagination or are used fictitiously.

Printed in the United States of America.

ISBN: 978-1-4269-5508-2 (sc)
ISBN: 978-1-4269-5509-9 (hc)
ISBN: 978-1-4269-5510-5 (e)

Library of Congress Control Number: 2011901036

Trafford rev.02/22/2011

www.trafford.com

North America & International
toll-free: 1 888 232 4444 (USA & Canada)
phone: 250 383 6864 • fax: 812 355 4082

Always And Forever 05, 16 2009

The least I can say about our story is that it is a bit uncommon. They were two young women who were absolutely inseparable and that since their early teenage years. They told each other then, that it was for always and forever, that nothing and nobody would come between them. One of them with black hair and a very soft white skin have on herself some beautiful round and fair size breasts. They are firm and they could fill my eyes and my hands, I was sure of that. She is my height, thin without being skinny, a person very enjoyable to hold in my arms. I strongly fell in love with her the first night we danced holding each other closely and tenderly. Neither one of us didn't care, not even a bit about the rest of the world at that time. The music was soft and we were both in another world, so much that we could make love right there and then on the dance floor among everybody. I have never felt that way in my whole life. To my surprise when she opened her mouth, she said; "You'll have to dance with my friend too."

I was expecting more something like; your place or mine? I told her right away.

"I only want you, I only want to dance with you, I only want to make love to you, I only want to live with you." "You don't know what you're talking about. You hardly know me." "Maybe so, but I know what I want in life, and I mainly know how I want her to be, that is what I found with you." "I appreciate what you're saying, but give yourself some time and in the mean time, dance with my friend, would you please?" "Then, it is only to please you. What is her name?" "Her name is Janene." "What is she doing in life other than being you're best friend?" "She's a nurse at the hospital." "And you didn't tell me what you are doing?" "I do the same thing at the same place." "Interesting ! You girls work the same hours?" "Not always!" "OK then, introduce me." "Let's go."

The crowd was dense and we had to walk to the table pushing one another to make our way through.

"To tell you the truth, I would rather take you to my bed than dance with you're friend." "Wait, you'll see. We have a lot of time, the night is young."

Once we got to their table, I thought I was in some kind of a dream. I was facing at that precise moment what I thought was the most beautiful woman in the world. The most pretty blond girl who existed on the face of the earth. They are just about the same size, but totally different one another in look. Her friend was sitting down with a man quite a bit older than her. She introduced him to me right away.

"Hi Danielle, you seem to have fun? Let me introduce you to this man. His name is John. He is a trucker and he travels across the country." "Nice to meet you John, I know that you know my brother." "Yes, yes I know him well."

So I said hi too and I shook his hand.

"Janene, I have a very nice young gentleman to introduce you too. I don't know yet what he's doing in life, but I can tell you that he's the best dancer I happened to dance with and you absolutely have to dance with him. He can dance anything you want too. Janene, this is James."

"No, no, I'm just a very ordinary dancer. Hi Janene, nice to meet you!" "Very nice to meet you James!"

That's what she said shaking and holding my hand in an unusual way. I felt a bit bad, because just a few minutes ago I just told the one I thought was the woman of my life that I love her. Who could imagine such a thing? Not that I was also in love with Janene, but I was definitely blown away by her beauty. Janene got up and asked Danielle to follow her to the lady's room.

"Where did you find this phenomenal guy?" "He was back there against the wall, hoping I supposed that a pretty girl smile to him.

He seemed to me very gentle, so I smiled back to him and I found myself happily in his arms. I believe that I'm in love with him and that he feels the same way with me." "But, you just met him. I can't blame you, I have to admit that he is very attractive." "That's what you think too?" "Usually, you don't have the same taste than me." "Usually you pick ordinary guys." "It's true that James is special." "What are you going to do with John?" "Which John?" "The one you got sat down at your table." "Ho, this guy, he is boring. You got to get rid of him. He doesn't know how to dance and he would always be gone on the road somewhere. Besides, I don't like to travel in big trucks." "Here is what were going to do. You're going to dance with James and stay on the floor for as long as you can. I'll sit with John and yarn until he's bored enough to get the heck out off our air. What do you think?" "It seems to be a good idea, but its going to be very boring for you too." "What can't we do for our best friend? Just bring me James back in one piece, that's all I ask."

During that time I was bored to death with John, who had nothing else to talk about than his delivery on time and how important it was. It was a real small world for a guy who travels across the country. I had only one thing in mind and that was to find myself into Danielle's arms again. The wait felt like a cold shower after such a nice time I had just experienced with her. John just spent I don't know how much time with the most beautiful girl I have ever seen and all he had in mind was his darn truck. No wonder that Janene tried to get rid of him. I just hoped that he didn't cost me to lose Danielle for the evening. I was relieved when I finally saw them coming back to the table. I was afraid that they wouldn't come back because of him.

"Here you are the two of you. I was getting a bit worried." "No, no, James, you'll have to know how to wait." "That's true Danielle, especially if we are sure that we are not waiting in vain." "Don't worry James, when we find gold, we keep it preciously. I think I found some tonight." "Ho yea! I hope you're right, because I think I found a treasure too, one I wouldn't want to be too long without." "James, if you want to please me now, you're going to take my friend to the dance floor." "Are you sure that you know what you're doing? I could make it a habit, you know?" "I hope so James, she is my best friend."

At that moment I had shivers. I was scared of what I just heard. Many questions came to my mind. Does she want to get rid of me already when she seems to be so fine in my arms? Does she want to test me by pushing me into her best friend arms? Such a beautiful woman! Does she want to push me away, because she's interested in somebody else? I looked at her intensely and I asked myself if I should simply refuse to go away. But how can I say no to someone I love and refuse her anything in such a short time? There was almost a supplication in her voice and Janene seemed to be so impatient to get on the dance floor with me. Maybe Janene just wanted to get away from this guy, the trucker. Maybe she's interested in me too when I think of the way she held my hand earlier. There was one thing I knew for sure and that is I didn't have much time for all the answers to my questions. What to do? I said; see you later Danielle and I took Janene by the hand and I brought her to the dance floor. I was a bit upset I must say. The band was playing a cha, cha, a music that puts me in a mood for dancing very quickly. We danced it with conviction and so we did with the next piece of music, a fast rock & roll.

"Wow! Danielle was right, you know how to dance." "Sure, a little! We should go back now and try to get our breath back." "There is no way, unless you are suffering." "I'm fine, but I don't want Danielle to think that I already abandoned her, especially with such a beautiful woman and her best friend above all. It's not that it is not fun, but, are you always that skin-tight?" "It's been long since I had the taste to hold someone like this."

"You're only an hour late and everything could have been totally different, if I met you first. I have to admit that you are very pleasant and extremely pretty, but I'm already in love with Danielle."

A mambo followed and I asked her if she knew how to do it hoping that her answer would be negative.

"Sure, it's my favourite dance." "No luck then, it's my favourite too."

There were very few people on the floor and only another couple knew how to dance it. People all around us were watching with envy, I could tell. As soon as the music ended, they applauded to the point that it was almost embarrassing. Janene jumped to my neck holding me tight, kissing me and saying that she couldn't dance like this since she had her last dance with her dance instructor six years ago. She had on a very pretty white dress with red buttons and shoes to match it. I thought at that moment that it was possible I could fall in love with her too in different circumtances. She had a nice sun tan on a beautiful skin, her hair is like gold and her eyes are of the nicest blue. She could, I'm sure make thousands of men dream of her. Her breasts are a bit smaller than Danielle's, but firm and pointing up. Her bump is neither too small and neither too big and her waist could make all the models of the world dream of it. It was enough to wonder why such a beautiful young woman was still single while thousands of men would like to marry her. It would be hard for me to dance a slow dance with her without being tempted to put ma hands on those cheeks. Thinking about slow dance the musicians thought it was time to slow down and it was a real sentimental one. I was lost in my thoughts with my observations about the one I was with on the dance floor when I remembered that I was forgetting the one I love. I felt bad and ashamed of myself.

"Janene, I have to join Danielle now." "No way, there is no way that I'll let you go before we finish this beautiful slow. Then Danielle will join us as soon as she got rid of this non sense guy at our table." "I don't understand, if you don't like the guy, why don't you just tell him to go away?" "It's not that simple, he is her brother's friend." "Ho, I see, she feels obligated. But if I understand well, you girls have tricked me into this."

Time went by and I found myself stuck in her arms surrounded by a couple of hundred peoples tight together on the dance floor. With her whole body Janene firmly stick herself against mine like a leech and I decided to give her a simple of what it could be like between us if it was possible. She took one of my hands and she pulled it down on her bump which seemed to me in fire. My member got bigger and I started to sweat and that really made me uncomfortable. At the moment when I was going to push her back, Danielle joined us.

"How are you doing the two of you? I'm please to see that you're doing well. Danielle put her arms around us and held us from behind me and the three of us finished the dance that way. Not only she pressed herself against me, but she also pulled Janene towards me, pinching me feverishly between those two pairs of wonderful breasts like a meat sandwich. Believe me that was something to warm me up, to say the least. We finally got closer to the end of that wonderful and memorable evening, one I'll never forget for as long as I live. Nevertheless I was not yet at the end of my sweats. I was not scared about my health, because I was definitely in good hands with these two lovely nurses. I'm a guy who is strongly built and in a super good shape physically, but I had again a fair number of questions concerning these two. What were these two beautiful young women really looking for? Are they single or married? The reality is not always what people say. That they were nurses I had no problem to believe it. The fact that they were best friends that too was not very hard to believe, but was there something more? Two of the same sex who goes together nowadays is not that rare and it is the same with the bisexuals. Usually women are looking for taller guys, which is not my case. I have no complex about it, because there is not much a tall guy could do that I couldn't. The fact is there are a lot of women who married tall guys because they were tall and handsome and they cried bitterly. The look and the height of a person don't guaranty happiness. Women especially should remember this. I have to stop questioning myself I suddenly realized.

I have to live the good time when it's there, otherwise I'll never see it. I still didn't know what they had in mind for the rest of the night. I knew though that what I had was better than I could ever dream of, that thousands of men would dream the same thing.

"What are we doing from here Danielle?" "What about you? Do you have any idea?" "All I know is that I'm not quite ready to say good night just yet." "Me neither James!"

"Me neither." "Janene said! What do we do then?" "Janene and I have a large apartment, something to drink and something to eat and we invite you if you like to come?" "I have a fairly nice house too with three bedrooms, a sauna and a Jacuzzi, so what now?" "We invite you first, are you coming?" "Not yet, but I will, I'm sure. How could I refuse such a nice invitation? Sure, I'll come, I'm following you. Don't drive to fast. I don't want to lose you. Danielle you should give me your address and your phone number just in case something happened, we never know, you know?" "That's true too but, I think the hazard made things right so far tonight." "It's true, but I don't want to take any chances." "Here James, see you in a bit."

The two of them gave me an unforgettable hug followed by a kiss and I went toward my car right away. They went to their car too and it seemed to me that they got into a deep conversation as soon as they left me. I started the vehicle right away and I drove it and parked it just behind their car. They got going and I followed them. They still seemed to me in a big discussion and I hoped that they were not going to fight over me. Ho how much I wished I could hear what they were saying. The worst that could happen as far as I was concerned is that one of them was jealous. It's possible I told myself, but yet again, I question too much. Happens what happens, I'll go to the end of this adventure. In the mean time in the other car something was going on.

"Janene, you have never liked the guys I was interested in or the ones who were interested in me." "It's true, but you have never met someone like him.

He is very gentle and polite, he dress nice, he dance magnificently, he's got a new car, which means that he's got a good job." "You forgot that he's got a house too. He seems very strong for a little guy, did you notice that too?" "That's true. When he held me in his arms, I felt that he's holding me good, that I was not going to fall. He is special that one, there is no question about it. You seem to love him a lot, but I know that I could love him too." "One thing is sure and that is I don't want any competition between us and no jealousy either. We never had and we cannot let that happen." "Danielle what ever happens, you'll always be my best friend." "You too, Janene!" "What are we going to do then?" "We shared him so far and it wasn't too bad, what do you think?" "I think, it was super." "He didn't seem to mind that either." "He was rather unwilling to stay on the dance floor with me at first." "What happened after?" "I held him back like you asked me to." "Rascal, it wasn't too hard for you, was it?" "It's probably the nicest mission you asked me to fulfill for you. He worried a lot about you though. I even believe that he is in love with you. I had a hard time to hold him back, you know? I think he danced with me to please you. He was quite afraid that it could displease you to stay on the floor with me. Should we keep sharing him?" "Yes! You'd do anything for me and I'd do anything for you, why not? We'll see what he thinks of it."

The two of them gave each other the high five in agreement. I followed them in an underground parking lot of a large condominium building where I parked in a guest area. They gave me another warm hug and I could see by their smiles, that they were pleased with my presence.

"Come James." Danielle told me. They grabbed my arms, one on each side and Danielle said; "Let's take the elevator that will take us to the sixth floor."

It was obvious that they were not women who live in misery. It was late in the night and we were alone so they weren't shy to take turns in kissing me all away up to their floor. It was obvious too that they didn't invite me just for a quick coffee or a cup of tea either.

But what ever happen I was ready for anything, any eventuality. Both of them were showing me their interest and I could appreciate that just as much from both of them even though I think I was in love with Danielle. I was like the words of a French song from Dalida that says; "Happy like an Italian when he knows he'll get some sex and some wine." Maybe I wasn't on the seventh heaven, but I'm sure I was at least on the sixth. We got out of the elevator and they invited me into a superb luxurious condominium. There is a forty-eight inches TV in a greatly furnished living room. They guided me to a very comfortable sofa and Danielle asked me.

"Would you like something to drink James?" "I will only if you girls take something too. I would like another long kiss from you Danielle." "Hin, hin, if you kiss me you'll have to kiss Janene too and the same way." "What? What is this plot?" "It is very simple James, it is that or nothing, but the choice is yours." "What is it? A kissing contest of some kind?" "No, it is just that we shared you all evening and we both found that very enjoyable. It is also that we both would like to continue, because we both love you very much." "Well, I was expecting almost anything, but certainly not this." "What were you expecting exactly James?" "I..., I was expecting maybe to finish what I started with you Danielle." "And when did you plan to finish what you started with Janene?" "There, well I'm sorry, but I didn't plan anything at all about that. What if it goes farther than a kiss?" "We are willing to share everything if you agree of course." "What would happen if I only have enough for one?" "When there is enough for one, there is enough for two. You know the dictum, don't you? If you can only give us one portion, I'm sure that we will be satisfied with it." "You're serious?" "Yes! If you can give me just half a portion and half a portion to her that will be fine too. Better yet you could make love to Janene tonight and to me tomorrow." "And you seem to be very serious?" "You're right, you can bet we are." "You girls being nurses, can you get me the blue pills at a better price?" "If that becomes necessary we'll take care of it, don't worry, we're not nymphomaniac. We don't want to kill you or hurt you in any way on the contrary, we'll take care of you like a baby, our baby." "Wow! I'm simply astonished. Forgive me, but I have a bit of a problem to digest all this. Where do we start?" "We made you sweat tonight, let's start with giving you a nice hot bath." "Here we are, I'm already in hot water. What a start!"

That made them laugh a good shot.

"Can you assure me that there will be no jealousy ever?" "Yes we can." They both agreed with a big smile. I started to sing a song I know, what made them laugh even more. Let go to swim my sweethearts, let's go all swim together."

When I entered this room I found out that it wasn't an ordinary bathroom. It was as big as a normal bedroom, a room ten feet by twelve with a tub six feet in diameter at least two feet high. When I entered I said;

"But this is not a bathtub, it's a swimming pool."

The two of them were undressed In no time leaving me with no choice, I had to move and there was no time to waste. I have to admit that I was still in an emotional shock. I had a hard time to believe that I wasn't dreaming on one hand and on the other I couldn't keep my eyes off those two beautiful naked bodies. I was totally in disbelieved and yet you know what they say; yes, seeing is believing. I don't think that a million dollars would have made me any happier.

"Come on, jump in James, we're going to take care of you. You too Janene, get in here."

Danielle got comfortably behind me while Janine took place in front. It was unbelievably enjoyable. I have never live through such a pleasurable thing in my whole life.

"Tonight James you can only look, you can not touch. Do you agree Janene?" "Everything is fine with me Danielle." "Just a minute there, this is not only mental cruelty, but it is also physical cruelty."

"What are you complaining about James? You're not well with us?" "I am extremely well Danielle, but it is nevertheless very cruel to look at those beautiful breasts in front of me and so close and not being able to touch them. Besides, I feel yours in my back without being able to see them. Come on let me touch them at least once." "What do you think Janene? Should we let him?"

"It's alright with me if you don't mind." "If that will please both of you then I would not intervene. Just once then!"

"I think I will make that just once last a very long time."

While I was playing with Janene adorable breasts and looking her straight in her eyes, Danielle grabbed me and started to mass gently but firmly this thing that was ready to explode at any time. At that precise moment I was confused, because I wasn't sure if I loved one more than the other. Then came the crucial moment when there was no way I could hold back. I was still holding those beautiful things in my hands when the explosion occurred. There was some for everyone especially for Janene who was in a position to get the most. She had some in her hair, in her face, in her eyes and if she'd opened her mouth at that moment, she would have been the first one to taste me. The only time I remembered I was that generous with this liquid is when I was only fourteen years old. It was then my first sexual experiences.

"It looks like you got an eye on me Janene?" "You're right love, I got some everywhere. You're a real seafood James." "It's good?" "It's salted." "Ho yea, I hope you like salt." "In a matter of fact, I do." "Good!"

I gently pulled on those two beautiful breasts and brought her closer to me and I gave her a tender long kiss. The ejaculation seemed to be endless to the point that I started to have a bit of a pain in the back of my head that I couldn't explain. I also felt a bit weaker and it scared me even though I was in good hands. I finally left Janene breasts and I turned around to face Danielle. I asked her if I could only touch hers once also and I gave her a long kiss. She knew that I was pleased with the pleasure she'd just gave me and that I appreciated it. During this moment of exaltation Janene pressed herself against me and ran one hand in my hair and tried to resuscitate me with the other hand. Then I went to sit behind Janene and I asked Danielle to pass me the shampoo.

"Danielle, we're going to give this beautiful blond girl a lovely bath, she really needs it, do you agree?" "Of course!" "You wash her hair and I'll take care of the rest, OK?" "Alright, wash everywhere, don't cut the corners." "Don't you worry, I always try to do things right."

"It's very nice to discover you James." "You like that?"

I took a bar soap and I started rubbing her back from her neck to her bump, what gave her shivers over her whole body. After rinsing her I went to the front where I let my hands slip from her throat to her pubis. I spent a lot of time on her breasts again. Danielle who didn't miss a thing said;

"Hey there, we said only once, you're cheating." "Not at all Danielle, I don't touch now I wash."

I let my hands travel all over her whole body and from time to time I also passed the back of my hand between Danielle's legs. She didn't complain about that one. Then I came back to Janene and this time I went where it teases the most, but then it was more than shivers, it was wiggles. I would go as far as saying, it was torture. I have to say that there I was cheating a little bit when I let one finger slipped in the opening of her intimacy. Her whole body was telling me; give me more. I muttered to her ear; "Sorry, I can't go any farther, I'm not allowed." "That's enough for me."

Janene said getting up very suddenly. I understood that there was a bit of frustration in her voice. After she got up she dried herself and said;

"I'm going to wait for you in bed."

"Do you think she's mad?" "Janene mad, never! Hungry maybe, but not mad."

"Well, I'm glad to hear that. I'm going to wash you quickly and we should join her before she falls asleep." "I agree." "Is she going to eat something?" "What she's hungry for, you don't find it in the cupboards and neither in the fridge." "I see, it's got to be my fault then. Let's hurry before she's cooling off."

We quickly got out of the tub, dried each other and walked rapidly to the bedroom. Janene was lying down naked on the bed, smiling and absolutely dazzling. She had one hand on one breast and the other one near her velvety pubis. Danielle who was holding my hand pulled me towards Janene and said;

"She's first, she works tomorrow."

When I got close to Janene I started to caress her with all of my knowledge hoping that it was good enough for the situation. I will only know if I can get her to have many orgasms. Her pubic hair was so blond that it looked almost invisible. I spent a long time kissing her deeply knowing that she was burning with desire. When I came down on her body I noticed that Danielle just beside us had taking a similar position that Janene was in when we entered the room. I went directly to the goal and I let my thirsty tongue and lips do what they were dying to do for many hours then. She didn't waste any time for coming again and again. She's going to drown me I thought, but she was so delicious, that I didn't dare to stop. Finally it was Danielle putting one hand in my hair indicated that it was time for me to stop. I got on my knees and Janene did the same in front of me kissing me and she said with tears in her eyes;

"It's been five years James, you are marvellous. Thank you." "There is no problem sweetheart. You're welcome anytime."

Danielle was about to cry too and I even think that she shed a few tears. I stretched myself down between the two of them without a word for few minutes and then Danielle whispered;

"James, she's sleeping. I'll cover her up and we'll go lay down in the other room."

I was almost sad to leave her behind. I came very close to come another time during this last workout. After Danielle had covered Janene she took me by the hand and led me to another room almost as luxurious. Just the bed is a bit smaller.

"Are you too tired now James? If you want to sleep I would understand." "We'll do like Janene if you want, we'll come first. We'll have a lot of time to sleep tomorrow. We rolled down the blankets and we jumped in the bed.

"Do you know that I'm waiting for this moment since I lift my eyes on you?" "Without lies?" "Of course, I never lie." "Never?" "It would have to be a real uncontrollable situation." "Can you give me an example?" "Sure, let say that I am a cop and I see someone who is ready to jump down a bridge, because he or she wants to kill herself and I ask her to come down saying with a lie that she wouldn't be persecuted. It's a good lie or a necessary lie, I should say." "Can you give me another example? Not now sweetheart! Right now I want to caress you until you fall asleep." "Alright, that's alright with me."

I gave her the same treatment that Janene received.

"Are you feeling good enough for a complete session?" "I certainly am, but I'm not a cheater." "I see that revenge is sweet to James' heart." "It is not revenge darling, it is faithfulness." "I agree, because I know you're right. I think I would have loved it." "Janene too ! Wait till tomorrow, this way no one could say that I got you the first day we met." "I want you so much." "Me too, believe it!" "Its true that many people think that it is wrong for a woman to give herself to a man on the first date." "Personally I think that the decision belongs to the two people involved and so are the consequences. You know that we never know. I might just be a guy who goes to the brothels." "No way, not you!" "There are good looking guys who are timid and go to those places."

At the same time I sat beside her and I said;

"Don't you worry this is not my case."

I kissed her one last time and we fell asleep in each other arms. It was our first night of love and I didn't forget the least detail. At around noon, Janene came to join us and said;

"I see that you guys deserted me." "Hi you!" "Good morning to both of you!"

"You were sleeping so well that we didn't want to wake you up." "It's true that I sleep like a baby who makes it through the night. I'll have to be put to bed more often this way. I'm going to take a bath, I feel sticky." "Put enough water for two, I feel the same way."

"Go ahead girls. I would like to sleep another hour if you don't mind. Don't let me sleep any longer than that though."

Danielle gave me a little kiss on the mouth and went to join Janene in the bathroom. I was thinking about the whole evening and the night; it's not a dream they're really here. I also new that they weren't lesbians, because it would have been impossible for a lesbian to see Janene in the state that she was, lying on the bed naked and not touching her. Then I fell asleep again. In the mean time these two had another plan in mind.

"Do you think it's possible Danielle?" "Of course it is. I think that I have enough now." "Are you sure?" "Yes, I am."

They came to wake me up at two forty-five just before Janene departure for her work. Janene came to give me a hug with a kiss and she quickly left. Danielle came to sit beside me on the bed and asked;

"What would you like to eat?" "It depends." "It depends on what?" "Well, if we're going to make love for the rest of the day I would certainly need a couple of eggs." "Are you sure that eggs are good for this?" "That's what they say. Do you know anything better?" "I will ask the doctor. How do you like them?" "Over easy with a pair of white toasts and a cup of tea with un sugar and no milk. I can do them if you like." "Give me a chance to try first and if you don't like them then you can make them yourself." "Go ahead then, but I have to warn you, I'm the worst client for the best cook." "What do you mean by that?" "I mean I don't eat everything, everywhere, anyhow, I'm very fussy and on top of everything I have allergies." "We'll learn to know you. I'm sure that there will be some compensation for the inconveniences. Things will work out." "I appreciate your understanding, thanks." "Breakfast is ready." "I'm starving. I didn't eat anything in the last twenty-four hours beside you girls." "I'm sorry; we didn't offer you anything to eat." "On the contrary, you offered me what was the best, but not for the stomach." "Mmmmm, they're good, exactly the way I like them. What about you, you don't eat?" "We ate while you were sleeping." "Why didn't you wake me up as I asked you?" "We both decided that you needed a good rest well deserved." "I see, it's nice of you. Thanks for the breakfast." "Ho, you're welcome."

We talked about nothing and everything and then the phone rang at around five thirty. Danielle picked it up.

"Allô!" "Allô Danielle, I can't talk too long, we're expecting an emergency at any minute now, but the result is negative. Say hi to James for me." "I will. That was fast, thanks."

Danielle put the phone back on its cradle and she seemed worried." "You've got bad news?" "No, on the contrary, it's good news." "Why do you look so worried then?" "I'm always like that when I have to take a quick and important decision. That was Janene. She said to say hi. You had enough to eat? Do you want some more?" "No, that was plenty, thank you." "What would you like to do now?" "If you could lend me a tooth brush and tooth paste, I'd like to brush my teeth and rinse my mouth then I'd like to wash a bit." "Go lay down a little and I'll run a bath."

"I'm I dreaming or you're always so sweet?" "It's nice to be ourselves for the person we love." "You love me, is that true?" "I don't lie either James."

I took her in my arms and I strongly kissed her. Then I threw myself on the bed and she went to the bathroom. When she came back to tell me that it was ready, I was already dozing. She helped me getting up by pulling on my arm and I went to jump in the tub. When I finished brushing my teeth I came back to the bedroom to find her lying on the bed. She was the most desirable and me, well, I was naked like a worm. Sorry no, all I was wearing were my glasses. I came closer to her and I started to undress her. With all of my heart I wanted to make love to her. With something else too, but I wasn't sure that was the best thing to do."

"Can you explain to me how it is possible to love a person or two so much in such a short time?" "No, in fact, I was asking myself the same question." "I want to make love to you, but I think that I should be tested first." "Why, do you think that you might have a disease?" "I don't know, I've never been tested for this." "I have to tell you James, I'm a virgin." "Seriously?" "I'm very serious." "Who could have believed such a thing? And you're twenty-four?" "I have never loved someone enough to give myself to him until now." "There is also the risk to get pregnant. I don't have any protection. I never thought myself to get in that position." "I thought that a nice looking guy like you would have sex every time he's going out." "This is the first time I go out in two years. I went out last night because it was a special occasion." "And what was the occasion?" "It was my birthday." "Seriously? It's true, you don't lie. We'll have to celebrate this, how old are you?" "I just turned twenty-seven." "Happy birthday then!" "Thank you!" "I want you to make love to me now." "Now?" "Now!" "Don't you think that I should be tested first?" "Well it's done." "What do you mean, it's done?" "I mean that it is already done. Janene and I asking you for forgiveness, but Janene brought a simple of your sperm to the laboratory and when she called earlier it was to tell me that the result was negative. You have no disease."

"But you girls stole from me." "I rather think that you gave it to us." "And how, I've never come that much since I was fourteen or fifteen. Well, that's a good news, but what to do to avoid pregnancy?" "Don't worry, I'm not in a dangerous period right now. Like one would say go in peace or come in peace." "Ok then may peace be with us."

During the time of this conversation my hands didn't stop undressing her and they were all over her shivering body. I felt the tension going up every time I was approaching her breasts and her low belly. It has been a long time since I was with a woman, because this is not something I give to everyone. I got on top of her and I kissed her tenderly while holding her left breast in my hand. With all my heart I wanted to give her the maximum of pleasure. I don't think I left any part of her body untouched. The hardness of her nipples was telling me a lot about the way she felt. She was all mine soul and body and I was fully aware of it. I made her come many times orally and I suddenly felt the need to position myself in her wonderful love nest, because I was ready to explode at any moment. I got on top of her again and in one time two movements, three shots in, it was gone. My fear was founded, because one more time I came prematurely. The engine that is supposed to give the most part of the pleasure and satisfaction to your partner just lost the best part of its power. Luckily the power lasted just enough to give her another orgasm.

I'm sorry, I wish I could hold it a lot longer." "Don't be sorry it was so good." "Believe me it could be much better. I got to find a way to make it last a lot longer for both of us." "I believe and I trust you." "If you want we can wash and start all over again." "I'd like to just lie beside you and chat. I feel so great in your arms and I love to hear you talk." "What do you want to talk about?" "Nothing and anything and what ever comes to your mind." "I wonder what Jeannette Bertrand would think of our story, a triangle." "She would probably be scandalized." "I don't think so. Do you know that she did a radio sex talk show for a long while?" "I didn't know that."

"I heard her say once on the air that more than fifty per cent of the sport world, more than fifty per cent of the artistic world and more than fifty per cent of the clergy was homosexual." "That is a lot of people. I didn't know that." "I am both ways since last night." "Ho no, don't you tell me that you're bisexual." "Don't make me laugh, I'm a guy who loves both of you. It's quite an experience and I hope it's not a one night story, because ladies I'm deeply in love with you both." "Don't mock me James, it would hurt too much." "I don't mock you Danielle, it's not my style, seriously, I love you and I believe I love Janene too very much. It makes me feel strange to say that though, I feel a bit like cheating both of you." "You must not feel guilty about this, we put you in this position and that is what we wanted." "When did you plan this plot?" "Last night! I always knew that I could share anything with Janene, but I never thought she could love the same man. This is the first time she likes my partner. It's actuality the first time she pays attention to anyone in five years." "What happened to her?" "She had a deep deception, but I'll let her tell you herself." "Sure! I'm sorry, I just wanted to understand. You girls are serious you don't mind the triangle?" "If you agree, we we'll be happy about it." "You didn't even ask me what I was doing for my living." "That is because we don't need your money." "I'm touched, really. So, it means when a woman asked, it's because she needs support? I don't need your money either, I make a good living." "What are you doing for work?" "I'm a journeyman carpenter, I build houses." "Janene and I talked about having a house built sometime on a big lot and we want at least three bathroom. If you ever build our house, just be sure of something, we don't want any favour, meaning no discount. We won't want to use you." "What ever, we'll talk about this when the time comes. What time is it?" "It is near midnight. We should dress up, Janene will be here within twenty minutes. I spent a very nice day with you James, I'm happy. I'm going to make tea and a snack for all of us." "Danielle, tell me that I'm not dreaming, I have trouble believing in that much happiness." "If you're dreaming, I'm dreaming too, but trust me, I rally lost my virginity today and I think that it couldn't have been with a better man. I always knew it would happen with a good guy." "I'm glad you waited for me."

With these words Janene was opening the door."

"Hi both of you, how are you doing?" "We are fine. What about you, did you have a good day?" "Yes! It was funny, most of them thought that I won the lotto. In a way they were right. Only the doctor guessed right, I even think that he is a bit jealous." "Jealous or not I want a hug from you and I'm not ready to let you go just yet."

I took Janene in my arms and I hold her real tight for a long time while I kissed her deeply. My idea was to taste that mouth, but also to make sure there was no jealousy between these two young women that I was then in love with. Contrary to what one could expect Danielle was happy for both of us. It was almost disarming. Everything happened so fast I had a hard time to assimilate all this. I hate jealousy and I hate cheating too. Both of them can ruin any relationship. It is jealousy that pushed Cain to kill his brother Abel.

"You know what Janene, it was James birthday yesterday." "And we got the gift, it's not fair really." "On the contrary, you girls made my best birthday ever. I still can't believe it. Tell me that it's not going to end tomorrow."

They looked at each other and then Janene said;

"Could you really believe that we want such happiness to end for us? We have to find a way to make this situation last forever." "We can not forget that the rest of the world will judge us very severely."

"We don't give a shit about the rest of the world. Do we judge people who sleep around left and right even married people?" "Don't get mad Danielle, it is just a reality that we cannot avoid." "Trust me James, we'll find a way. Where there is a will there is a way."

"Ho, I trust you and I'm sure that between the three of us we'll find a solution and a way to be happy in this dirty world."

"Well, I'm tired, I'm sleepy and I'm going to bed. I'll see you tomorrow. Good night James! Good night Janene! Don't go to bed too late."

Danielle gave us both a hug and a kiss and went to bed. I excused myself to Janene and I followed her to the bedroom where I helped her to get in bed. I also gave her a tender kiss and I told her that we'll see each other in the morning. After I covered her nicely with the blankets I left the room. I fear that the worst Monday in my life was coming up for me. Back to the kitchen Janene started to clean the dishes that were used during the day and I asked her;

"Where is the tea towel?" "There, beside the fridge, but you don't have to, I can handle this." "Take advantage of me, it wouldn't happen that often, especially with two women in the house. Let me do it, you already have a full day work behind you, besides, I like to be near you. I spent most of the day in bed." "You had a good time?" "I had an absolute gorgeous day." "I was forgetting, happy birthday."

That's what she told me putting her arms around my neck and kissing me with her languishing lips and her delicious tongue.

"What do you want to do James, watch a movie or go to bed?" "I better go to bed, I have to work tomorrow." "Ok then, let's go."

After taking a bath we walked to her bedroom where she opened the door and turned on the light and then I stopped her. I took her in my arms and I brought her to the bed which seemed to be really nuptial. She was all smiles and inviting so there I gently laid her down. We undressed each other looking in each other eyes. I put little kisses all over her face and then down on her breasts and then finally all over her body. She did the same with me which brought us both to a complete ecstasy. We gave ourselves to one another in a very complete way. I thought we both just found the kingdom of heaven. "Who when he had found one pearl of good price, went and sold all that he had, and bought it." Matthew 13, 46. We fell asleep in each other arms and woke up at seven-thirty in the morning. Danielle who woke up and felt lonely came to join us at four, but she was very careful not to wake us up. To this day I wonder if there is anything more scary than the thought of losing such happiness. Janene who was still in my arms kissed me saying, good morning.

"Wait a minute beautiful; I have bad breath in the morning because of my sinuses problem. I'll go wipe my nose, rinse my mouth and I will be back in a hurry. Wait for me."

"How did it go?" "It was super Danielle, I'm so happy. How did it go for you?" "It was good, but not extraordinary, although I think it was my fault." "I told you before, remember? The first time we are scare that it might hurt even though it's not always the case. It depends a lot on the man delicacy and gentleness."

"You must be right, because everything was fine until the penetration. I just felt a little pinch and that put an end to the pleasure immediately." "Welcome to the deflowered girl's club my dear friend. It will be better next time. You'll have a chance to catch on with me, because on my next long weekend of four days I'll go see my parents and tell them about our new man." "You don't think that you should wait a bit longer? Especially not if you want to tell them the whole truth. You know if you want it or not our families will put some shadow on our happiness. None of them will understand what we are living through." "What ever they say Danielle none of them can stop me from living this wonderful new life and I hope it will be the same for you." "Always and forever, only death can stop us."

The two women were doing high fife and laughing when I entered the room.

"How are you doing both of you? I'm I interrupting something?" "On the contrary, you are our continuation, but what took you so long?"

"Ho, I made a few phone calls to prepare my men for work and free myself until noon. That's what you girls make me do." "Janene will go away and let us alone for four days soon."

"She leaves us already, I'm going to miss her. Not that it is any of my business, but where will she go?" "In Gaspé to visit her parents." "Ho yea, I hope she's not going to tell them about us. I think it's too soon." "It's not too soon if we are all sincere and serious." "I am."

"Me too." "Which means that it's not too soon. I will tell them next week."

We all gave each other the high five followed with a kiss.

"I don't want to tell you what to do Janene, which means, I will talk to you in parables as for what concerns your parents. You know that gas was very high lately and people didn't really have a fit about it. Do you know why?" "Why gas was high or why people didn't have a fit about it?" "Why it didn't have a fit about it. You see when Jos Clark raised gas by twenty-five cent a gallons a few years ago, people was scandalized and his government was brought down because of it. Last summer gas went up eighty cents a litre which is three dollars and sixty cents a gallon and there was no crisis. Today gas came down to ninety cents a litre and people go fill their tanks with a smile. I just want you to think about this hoping that you will understand on time. This is a nine hundred miles trip return so I hope that you're going to take the train." "I had in mind to go with my car." "Think about it, two days to travel and two days to rest, it doesn't leave you much time to visit." "On the train it's tiring too." "But at least you can sleep on the train." "I'm going to miss my car." "You can always rent one." "Not in this back country! Don't you parents have a car? All I'm asking is that you're coming back in one piece." "I'm glad you're concerned, but what ever I decide, I'll be careful."

"Hay, you two, you must be getting hungry?" "Yes Danielle, you must be the most motherly of all of us. That's alright, this way I won't miss my mom too much." "You don't live with your mom anymore, do you?" "Are you kidding me? I left home when I was sixteen. Do you want me to make you some granny's crepes?" "What is this?" "Good crepes that I learned to make from my mom. It's one of my specialties. I love them a lot with pole syrup." "What is this again?" "It's another one of my specialties. I like it better than maple syrup." "Wow, that must be good?" "Another time maybe, because you wouldn't have time to make your syrup this morning."

They had their night robes on and all I had on was my underwear so I had to dress not to show up at the table almost naked.

"We have corn flakes, some rice krispies, and oatmeal, all of this is good for your health." "Do you have some fresh white bread?" "Yes, why?" "That's what I would like with milk and sugar." "That's another one of your specialties?" "Nothing is special about that, but I like it." "You're funny."

We took our breakfast talking about all kind of things but nothing in particular. I had to hurry when noon came, because I had no choice, work was out there waiting for me. I wouldn't have felt too good either with these two pretty women until I was shaved again. So I kissed them both with passion and I promised them to come back as soon as possible.

James before you go please give us your phone number." "Here it is." "What is the name of your company?" "It's called; Reliable Constructions and Fiab Enterprises." "That sounds reliable." "It is and so am I. I'm sorry, but I have to go, see you soon sweethearts."

I left them, but not without having a feeling of emptiness. I had just spent two days extremely enjoyable and fully appreciated. Only one thought came to haunt me and that was concerning polygamy, knowing that it was forbidden and illegal in Canada. I knew too that it is allowed in certain religions, but I'm totally and definitely against any kind of religion. I just knew that it won't be easy. I knew too that in Utah there are a few sects where it is permitted, but again it's not Canada. We are not at the end of our troubles, I thought. I had to stop thinking about that for a while.

I had some business to take care of. I had men to put to work and the customers rarely understand you being late no matter the reasons. Even though I have good workers the boss is the boss and he is the one to blame and the one to congratulate, but above all he has to be responsible. At that point I haven't had the time to delegate work or any body to replace me.

On my way to work that day I heard on the radio that two men, two church leaders near Vancouver just got arrested and charged for polygamy. I thought that the timing was quite strange, to say the least since I was wondering how in the world I could marry both of them.

Chapter 2

"Allô boss! What happened? You have never been late in two years?" "Well, I kind of celebrated my birthday this time." "Ho yea, happy birthday!" "Thank you. Is the drywall in?" "Not yet, but the windows and doors are in place in the three houses." "Well, we are going to install them this afternoon then. What about finishing trims, are they in?" "No, they should be here very soon though." "That's good, let's go to work now."

I finished that day that seemed endless. When I arrived at my house my mom and one of my sisters were there waiting for me.

"What happened to you? I tried to phone you for the last three days." "I'm sorry mom, I should have called you." "You're not reasonable. Where were you? You weren't home." "I wanted to get away from everything and then I forgot everything even my birthday."

"She was that pretty?" "Yes Céline, she is pretty and very pretty, believe me. I'll tell you about it another time."

"You were not at work this morning either and nobody knew where you were." "I just about called the cops on you, you know?" "Ho, I wouldn't have like that mom. I wouldn't have wanted to be disturbed especially by the cops. You'll have to get through your head mom that I'm old enough to live my life the way I want it no matter what you think. I didn't want to worry you, it's just that I was too captivated and I didn't think about calling you, that's all." "You must have a thousand messages on you voice mail." "I would like to invite you for supper, but I have nothing ready. If you want to I can take you to a restaurant." "It's not necessary, our supper is ready at home. Happy birthday son and next year make sure I can talk to you on your birthday."

"Happy birthday brother and be careful." "Thanks Céline, I'm going to call them all now. It's going to take a couple of hours." "For sure!" "Again, I'm sorry, forgive me. I'll see you soon."

Both mom and Céline took off and I went to listen to my messages.

"Happy birthday James, it's your little sister Marcelle." "James, it's me, your mother, call me as soon as you can." "Happy birthday little brother, it's me, Francine." "Happy birthday James, your sister Diane here." "Happy birthday James it's me Carolle, big kisses for your day. James, it's me again, your mother, give me a call, would you?." "Happy birthday, it's me, your friend Murielle." "Happy birthday, it's just your brother." "It's me my love. I miss you already, Danielle who miss you a lot. I kiss you. Bye ! " "Here's Rolland. I have details to discuss with you. Monique wants to change the color of the cupboards. Give me a call when you can."

That went on for another twenty minutes. We still like to know who called and who didn't. The thing is that I had something else than the birthday wishes on my mind. Even so I had to make at least twenty calls to thank them for their wishes. None of them though could have wished me a birthday like the one I just lived through. Although, the more I think about it the more I get scared. I who is ordinarily never scared of anything. I was afraid to have to move out of my country, afraid to be obligated to join a religion to be able to marry the women I love. I was also afraid that one or the other or even the two of them get discouraged from the troubles that were awaiting us, but it was also in my nature to trust in life, in my destiny which served me good so far. After an hour and a half I was finally done with those calls and I received a call from Céline who was intrigued with what was going on with my life.

"Hi you! You're finally done with your phone calls?" "Finally, yes!" "I tried to call you many times already. For what I concluded you had a nice weekend?" "Very nice thank you! It was beyond all expectations Céline." "I understood that you met someone?" "Not one, but two!"

"Two what? I didn't met one, but two women and I don't want to talk about it on the phone." "I understand. When can I see you?" "Give me a minute to check my agenda. Wednesday if you want, I'll come and have supper with you." "I got that, come right after work." "I'll be there, good night."

At ten thirty that night I was in bed and I tried to sleep, but it was useless. Everything I lived through in the last three days was flashing back in my mind. I know very well that I need sleep to be able to function properly the next day. At twelve thirty I got up and I decided to make a phone call.

"Hi, Danielle here!" "Danielle, it's me and I need a nurse, I cannot go to sleep and I don't have any sleeping pill." "It's you, my love." "Do you know another way to make me go to sleep? I'm a person who needs his seven hours a night to function properly the next day." "I think you did pretty good in the last two days." "Did you have a good evening?" "Yes, but all the girls asked what's happening to Janene and I." "We can read happiness and distress on people's face, you know that, don't you? You're happy and people can tell. I'm happy about it."

"Well, I'll let you go. I understand that you need to sleep. You can make yourself an herbal tea and read until your eyes can't stand it anymore. That will help change your mind." "Well, thank you and say good night to Janene for me" "I will tell her" "Good night to you too, I love you both and I kiss you."

It was two thirty when I finally gave up thinking about all this. I felt like I slept about ten minutes when the alarm clock woke me up at seven thirty. I felt very heavy and I dragged myself to the bathroom where I got better after a hot shower. I took a quick breakfast and I went to work where there were many tasks waiting for me. When noon came I free myself from my workers to make an important phone call.

"Allô! Is that you Janene? How are you?" "I'm well and what about you James?" "I'm fine, thank you." "Could you finally sleep?" "Yes, but just a few hours. I miss you two." "We miss you too. I'm leaving Thursday morning for Gaspé." "Already?" "That's me, I don't drag things." "Do you really think you're doing the right thing?" "Don't worry, I know what I'm doing." "I would like to spend a night with you before you leave if you like of course?" "Of course I want, it will be wonderful if you can." "I will wait for you in the same parking lot when you come home. Is Danielle home?" "No, I'm sorry, she's gone shopping." "Well, say hi to her for me and I'll see you Wednesday night. I got to go now, I love you and kiss you like you know, bye."

Wednesday at five thirty I was entering my sister's home at the set time, but I just knew that it was mainly to satisfy her curiosity. She welcomed me with a hug and a kiss on each cheek. Her favourite meal, meat sauce spaghetti and matched potatoes were on the menu. If there is one in my big family who can understand my situation without judging too much, she's the one. We ate and then I helped her to do the dishes. Then started the bunch of questions.

"Now you're going to tell me what is going on with you James, I have to admit, I'm very curious." "Before I say anything you'll have to promise me to keep all this for yourselves." "I promise. I understood that you met two different pretty women. Don't tell me that you don't know which one to choose from?" "If that was the only problem, there would be no problem at all." "What do you mean by that? I don't understand." "I didn't make two encounters, but rather one encounter of two gorgeous women. Not only they are very pretty, but they are also very kind and intelligent." "What are they doing for a living?" "They are both nurses at the hospital." "You're going to be in good hands." "Who are you telling it to?" "But the thing is that I am already." "Already? What do you mean?" "I mean that I am already in their hands." "You didn't waste any time." "You're mistaking, they didn't waste any time. I just let them carry me in a whirlwind of incredible love and a new world of extraordinary happiness for me." "Would you have changed to the point of accepting unfaithfulness now, you who were disgusted by it.

I'm still disgusted by it Céline, it is just that there is no unfaithfulness at all." "You'll have to choose between the two or cheat on one or the other." "This is what its nice about the whole thing, I don't have to choose and I don't have to be unfaithful. I love them both and they are both in love with me. Now you're playing with my nerves, you're mocking me, right?" "Not at all, I'm telling you just the way it is." "Now I'm lost. I don't understand a thing you're telling me." "Let me start all over for you. They are best friends, they felt in love with me and I love them both, it's that simple." "Han, han, it's not simple at all, because soon or later jealousy will kick in and that will be a nightmare for all of you." "I checked that out already, they are happy for one another each time I kiss one or the other." "And you are flying like a bird." "Apparently the male bird only has one female in his life." "What a story! What are their names? One is called Janene and the other one is Danielle. Tonight I'll see Janene, because she's leaving tomorrow for four days. She going to see her parents and she will tell them about us three. Then I'll have four days to get to know Danielle a bit better." "Now you understand why it's best not to talk to anyone about all this, for now anyway." "It might be best not to talk to anyone ever about this." "The truth will come out soon or later." "I think you're not at the end of your troubles my brother." "I think so too, but I also think that it's worth it." "I hope so for you." "For what they both said, it wouldn't even matter if I was naked like a worm or poor like Job." "You hit them right in the eye like bull's-eye." "You don't know how right you are. I'll have to go soon, they finish working at midnight." "Do you mean you already sleeping with them?" "Yes, it was love at first sight for all of us." "Be careful, it could be hit and hurt at first sight too." "If it's always like last weekend it will be just marvellous Céline, take my word for it. I never imagined something that great. I got to go now though, I wouldn't want them to wait for me or to worry." "So you really love them. Good luck!" "Thanks and good night." "Good night too and thanks for coming." "It was my pleasure, thanks for supper too."

I got in my vehicle and I traveled towards my love ones' place. Streets were deserted and that allowed me to get there a bit earlier than they did. While waiting I relaxed by listening to a few good songs on the radio. As soon as I saw them coming in their little car I got out of mine and locked the doors, then I walked towards them in a hurry. Janene came out of the car first and came to jump in my arms. She held me real tight like she hasn't seen me for ages. She kissed me in a way I could tell she was really in love. When she finally let go I looked her straight in the eyes and I said;

"Allô Janene." "Allô James."

"Allô James." "Allô Danielle. How are the two of you?" "I think Janene was a bit afraid not to see you before her departure." "Why was she afraid? I only have one word." "Yes, but as you know anything can happen." "That's true, but we can't always be afraid." "What about you James, aren't you afraid sometimes?" "You're perfectly right, I'm afraid even at this moment that all this could just be a dream." "I'm afraid too that this could fall apart." "Don't fear Danielle, I love you both and I don't think anything could change this." "I hope you're telling the truth James from the bottom of my heart." "We should go up there now, you know that the walls have ears, don't you?"

Danielle was a lot less enthusiastic that night and I came to the conclusion that it was because she knew I was spending the night with Janene. She always been the same to this day, she doesn't want to get in the mood when she knows it's not her turn to have sex. I can understand that. I told them that I couldn't stay up too late that I have to work in the morning.

"I have to get up early too, my train is leaving at nine." "Then we should take a quick bath and hit the bed right away." "You don't want to eat anything?" "Nothing from the cupboards anyway, I had a big meal at my sister." "You two go ahead, I'll take mine later, I have a lot of time."

Janene went to the bathroom and I went to sit with Danielle in the living room for a few minutes.

"Yell at me when it's ready Janene." "Don't worry, I will.

"You look like you're not feeling too good Danielle? Is something wrong?" "I always worry when Janene leaves by herself for a trip." "Ho, that's what it is, mother hen. Janene is an adult full of good senses and I think you're worry for nothing." "I know what you're saying, but it's beyond me, I can't help it." "If you want to, I wont leave you alone and I'll come and spend time with you." "Well, I hope so."

"It's ready James." "I'm coming."

"Are you going to bed right away?" "No, I'm not sleepy and I'm going to watch a good movie." "See you later then, I'll come to say good night."

I ran to the bathroom and I jumped in the soapy hot water with whom I believe to be the prettiest woman in the world. Of course after I was undressed.

"Man, this is hot. How can you?" "We get use to it very quick." "If I was a rooster you could pull the feathers out off me very easily." "You are our rooster, but we wont pluck you, don't worry, at least, it's not our intention."

I shut her mouth with a deep kiss while I was holding her tightly in my arms. Then I washed her from head to toe taking my time on the spots that please both of us. When she fell clean enough she did the same thing to me. What a pleasure! Great happiness! I suggested that we make love right there in the water and she sat right away on what she loves particularly. I tried with all my strength to hold back, because I wanted the pleasure to last for her especially and for myself too, but unfortunately, the stupid thing exploded way too soon. I was certain this time she wished the love making would have last a lot longer. I knew then that I had to find a way to fix this situation before it causes emotional trouble for both of us. It's was true that it was all new for me. It was true also that she is very pretty and drives me crazy, that she excites me to a very high level. It was true that with Danielle it was very tight and stimulating. It was true too that I wanted to give both of them way more pleasure, at least as mush as they can endure. As soon as tomorrow, I told myself, I'll make an appointment with a psychologist.

"Janene, working in a hospital you must know a psychologist?" "Yes, I know one, it's a she. You have a problem?" "Yes, I have a holding back problem." "What do you mean?" "I just wish that I could have held it back another twenty or thirty minutes longer, not you?" "Yes, but I thought it was normal. You're young, I'm pretty, it's all new, I think it could get better with time." "I don't want to wait any longer. I want to give you both a lot of pleasure, not in a year or so. I want to give you a lot of pleasure as soon as possible." "What a caring person you are. I love you so much James. I am in love with you and I know that I will be happy with you forever." "I love you too Janene and I don't want that to stop ever. I think we should go to sleep now."

We got out of the tub and having dried each other, Janene put on her night robe and I put on a large towel. Then we went to say good night to Danielle.

"How's the movie?" "It's good." "Do you mind put it on pause for a minute? I would like to say good night to you the proper way." "Sure I can."

"Good night Danielle, sleep well." "Janene, I will take you to the train station tomorrow morning." "Is that true, I'm so happy. Don't worry, everything will be fine." "I know, but you know me, if something bad happen to you." "I'm telling you, nothing bad will happen to me." "I know you're right, I worry a lot." "What was to happen to me happened last weekend and I'll let nothing and nobody change a thing about it, believe me. I'm gone, good night."

Janene went to her bedroom and I wished Danielle good night my way. Then I went to join Janene who was not ready to go to sleep just yet. So I gave her the oral treatment, which became sort of one of my specialties. She's doing not too bad either. That give me another erection even stronger than the first one which allowed me one more penetration, more satisfying for both of us.

Morning came very quick though for the three of us who were around the kitchen table at seven fifteen. Our mother hen had already prepared a bunch of things. Coffey, tea and toasts were already served. It is surely different for me who live alone for more than eleven years. I sure can appreciate it even though I had no complaints to make about my life style. We mainly talked about Janene's trip and how she should tell her parent about us. I told them about my conversation with Céline that went pretty good. From one thing to another it was time for me to go already, but it was not without a bit of sadness. I don't like tears and neither difficult separation. I gave them both a hug and a kiss saying that I'll see them soon. It was hard. Only Janene was smiling and she said with a good reason;

"Hey, you guys, I'm not going to a funeral and I'm not going forever. I'll be back Sunday night, I promise." "Have a good trip Janene. I'll see you when you're back." "Well I hope so, I'll be fine."

"Have a good day Danielle, if you want I'll come tonight so you're not too lonely." "I would appreciate it, but only if you can." "Of course I can, thanks to God I don't have any other women."

That made them laugh a good shot and it was quite good at that moment. Then I slowly went on my way. Danielle took Janene to the station and I went to work. Janene who seemed sure about herself had butterflies in her stomach anyway, but I knew she could take care of the situation. She told us that what ever they say, it wouldn't change a thing about her position regarding our relationship. When the night came she phoned Danielle and she phoned me to say that she had a very good trip. She also said that her parents were in a good mood to that point. She said she will keep us informed as things go. At twelve thirty that night, I was back with Danielle.

"You're still sad, you're not reasonable, do you know that?" "I just hope her parents wouldn't be too hard on her. You know that people in the country don't think the same way we do." "I know, but Janene is a big girl and I'm sure she could handle them." "You must be right and we should go to bed and talk until we fall asleep. I appreciate you're coming, you know?" "Yes I do, but all the pleasure is for me. I love being with you. When do you have a weekend off again?" "At the end of this week I'll have two days off." "That's great I never work on Saturday and I have all my weekends off normally. I only work Sundays if it's really necessary." "Are you from seven days Adventist?" "I'm against all religions and I think it is the largest slavery ever invented. People kills in the name of their religion and a lot of them believe it's the will of God. They killed Jesus for the same reason." "You seem to know what you're talking about." "Are you religious yourself?" "Janene and I are catholic from birth, but we're not practicing. I don't know what really happened, but we both stop going to church." "The routine can become boring. I was born catholic too, but just like little puppies, one day my eyes were opened and I never went back. Puppies take about twelve days, it took me eighteen years." "But you believe in God, don't you?" "Me and God are one." "The priest in my dad's village would say that you just have blasphemed and my dad too." "It proves only one thing and that is that they don't know the word of God. Do you have a bible?" "Yes, I have it there somewhere on the bookshelf." "As soon as tomorrow, you should read John 17, 21-23. It is and it was one of Jesus prayer that we become one with God." "Why not now? I am curious and I would like to sleep well." "Alright, but we have to be reasonable, I work early tomorrow."

She got up and went to get the bible, Louis the Second, my favourite.

"Let me look here, you said John?" "John 17, 21-23. Let me read this for a minute. But you're absolutely right James." "One of the greatest and possibly the most important message from Jesus is in Matthew 24, 15." "The reader will understand." "In French it's a bit more specific. It's said; "May the reader be careful when he reads." That means that the traps, the lies are in the writing, the bible. There is where we have to look and no where else." "But James, the bible is the book of the truth." "Yes Danielle, but the truth about the lies too. I will explain this to you another time, if you want.

That's what I like to do on Saturdays, the last day of the week, the Sabbath day and the day of the Lord." "Why not on Sundays?" "Because I don't want to contradict God Who said in his law; Keep the last day of the week holy. Not the first day, but the last day. You can read it in Exodus 20, 8 – 11. There is a great promise to the one who obeys the law. I don't want to contradict Jesus either, who said that not the least stroke of a pen will disappear from the law for as long as the earth and heavens exist. It's written in Matthew 5, 17 -18." "Let me see. But this is all true. Wow! That's something. But, this is not what we were taught. We were taught that Sundays you will keep serving God." "There you are. What is Sunday?" "The first day of the week." "A four year old child could tell the difference. I made a little song on the subject." "What is it?" "They deceived me, they lied to me on the Sundays morning. They deceived me, they lied to me and I didn't take it one morning. The Lord said the Sabbath day is Saturday, the last day of the week. I wonder for whom is the Sunday." "Hay, that's cute." "Thanks Danielle. I'd like to go on for hours, but I need to sleep now. One more thing Danielle if you want?" "Go ahead, I love that stuff." "Are you serious?" "This bore and shock most people." "Not me, I like to discover." "Well, I'm glad it doesn't fall in deaf ears. If you want to next time you talk to your dad ask him if he calls his priest father." "I'm sure he does, but why?" "Because Jesus forbidden his disciples to do it. Please read Matthew 23, 9, would you?" "And call no man your father upon the earth: For one is your Father, which is in heaven." "Wow! My father will surely fall on his bump." "Ask him just to see his reaction." "I will." "I can't wait to see yours." "My what?" "Your reaction following the reaction of your father. I kind of know what he's going to say." "Ho yea, and what is it?" "I'm not telling you. I'm going to write it down and hide it then you'll see it after you talked to your dad." "Alright, I'll call him this weekend." "We got to sleep now." "I feel so much better James, it was really good to speak with you. I'm not sad anymore and my worries went away. I was a bit depressed, you know?" "Yes I know, but the word of God is very powerful. I have a favour to ask you." "What is it? I'll help you if I can." "I would like you to get me an appointment with a psychologist at the hospital." "Do you have a problem that we should know about?" "I have a problem that you both know about." "I don't understand, what is it?" "I almost always have a premature ejaculation and I want to fix that problem and soon is not soon enough." "I'll do better than that, I will require for you if there is a method or medicine and I'll let you know. What do you say?" "I'll say this is wonderful. Thank you very much. Good night

Danielle." "Good night James, I love you." "I love you too."

After hugs and kisses we fell asleep and woke up at seven in the morning. After a good breakfast I left her to go to work. In Gaspé near the village where I was born myself, it was a total different story. Janene was discussing with her parents especially her mom who cries very easily and can get very hysterical.

"Mom, Danielle and I know each other for more than ten years now, and were going to get married possibly this year." "You and Danielle to get married? Tell me that I'm dreaming, that's got to be a nightmare. A lesbian in my family! Danielle dragged you into this? I just know that you weren't born like this." "Be careful how you talk about her mom, she's my best friend and she always will be."

The mother Anne Marry started to cry and her husband Rene asked Janene to go take a little walk outside to give him time to calm down his wife.

"You're not going to cry all day, are you? We only see our daughter once or twice a year and I would like that to be a bit happier." "If she's going to marry another woman, she's not my daughter anymore." "Come on, calm down, would you, you're saying stupidities. Janene will always be our daughter. I trust her, she's very intelligent and I will always love her what ever she does with her life." "What are we going to do? The news will spread all away around here.

What a scandal! Everyone will look at us like dirt." "You always exaggerating things, we're not the first ones and we're not going to be the last ones either, believe me. My dad often said; "Life is high on legs." Which probably means that anything can happen. Janene is coming back, stop crying, would you?" "How could we congratulate her like we're supposed to do?" "We'll do our best."

"Janene, my sweet daughter, did you rally think this over? I want you to know that what ever you do, you'll always be my favourite girl." "I know, I'm the only one you have." "Yes, but I'll always love you." "I know dad, you're an angel, I love you a lot too." "When do you plan to get married?" "Probably in the summer, we didn't choose a date yet." "Can we ask you not to spread this around here?" "You can, but it is useless, because news have no frontier nowadays. Almost everything is known the same day."

"We have to keep this secret Janene, keep a lid on it." "What about you mom, can you keep the secret? I'll bet that you'll be the first one to talk about it."

"It won't surprise me either."

"Are we invited?" "Of course you are, we're not that wild. does that mean you're accepting the situation?" "Do we have any choice?" "Now that you are settled down I'm going to tell you the whole truth." "You're not going to tell us that you're going to create a club of those girls, are you?" "Don't be ridiculous mom, it's an all different story." "What are you going to tell us now? I think I heard enough for today."

"Would you keep it quiet for a minute Anne and let her say what she wants to say?" "Danielle and I are getting married alright, but it's not to one another. We are both getting married to a man." "So you're not lesbians then?" "Neither one of us is. It's not because we don't sleep around left and right with all kind of different people and that we love each other that we are necessarily lesbians. I know that they catalogued us that way, because we are best friends and that we live together and that we are still single at twenty-five, it's unfair." "But why did you say you were?" "I never said such a thing mom that was your own conclusion. All I said is that we were getting married and it's true, but I never said that we were getting married to one another. It is possible though that we're getting married the same day." "It's kind of strange that you both found someone to marry at the same time." "Danielle was just an hour ahead of me." "That is very strange! What is the name of yours?" "His name is James Prince. He's a real prince." "Why didn't you bring him over?" "He's very busy with important work." "What is he doing for a living?" "He builds houses."

"That's a good trade and it's good everywhere." "You got it right dad. He's a great man and I am deeply in love with him, otherwise, I wouldn't even be here, especially not at this time of the year." "Danielle also found someone? What is his name?" "That is the whole point mom, he's the same man." "What? You both love the same man?" "Yes mom and Danielle found him. We're both deeply in love with him and neither one of us wants to let him go. Neither one of us wants the other one to suffer from his absence and this is why we decided to share him like we always shared everything before." "Wow! That's quite some news and it's much more acceptable than a marriage between women. But you girls are going to kill the poor man." "Don't worry mom, we are nurses and we will take care of him. He didn't complain so far, on the contrary." "You guys are going to meet some troubles along the way with the authorities." "We know about it. It's crazy, isn't it? A man can have fifty girlfriends and have with them hundreds of kids who will become the state kids for most of them without been bothered by the law, but if a man has two wives and a dozen kids that he's taking care of, he's a criminal." "You got to remember that the man who makes kids all over the country could be charged for alimony." "Not necessarily mom!" "What do you mean?" "I mean that the father can't be charged if the mother declares the father unknown." "He would have to be not too paternal."

"Dogs don't care about their pups and they are ready to serve females any time anywhere. Our man is not like that, he's a good man who will take care of us and he will do anything to make both of us happy."

"Well Janene, we just got to congratulate you and wish you the best and a lot of happiness. If you need anything, don't hesitate to let me know." "We have all we need dad, we only needed understanding from both of you. Thanks dad, mom! Unfortunately I have to leave tomorrow. I'm working on Monday morning. I hope there is no storm in the forecast. It is important that I'm in, otherwise there will be some surgeries postpone and it could cause people's death. Almost all hospitals in Quebec are short of staff, mainly doctors and nurses."

"You deserve all the best Janene no matter how you get it." "Make sure your car start in the morning dad, I can't afford to miss the train, you know?" "I know, don't worry sweetheart, you'll be there on time. Sleep well." "Thanks for everything dad."

The first obstacle of our adventure was now behind us so we had to concentrate on the next one. The three main reasons for divorces in life are money, children and religion. I didn't worry about money, because they had enough for all their needs and both of them had a job security and well paid above all. They were assured also of a good pension at the end of their mandates. I was making a good living myself even though the risk is a lot higher in business. It's not always easy to force someone who doesn't want to pay to do so, although I was not worrying about my financial situation. About family I wasn't too much worried either, but I still needed to know Janene intentions on that. I also needed to know what were her views on religions. As far as Danielle is concerned everything was settled. I knew that there is no more motherly than her and I knew too, that she likes my way to see things about religions and the slavery that they impose. I was not too worried either about Janene on that subject, because I had an ally with Danielle on my side. I was really happy with Danielle's reaction, because I'm always pleased to tell someone about my bible discoveries. On Friday night I was back again with Danielle to spend the night. To this day Friday night is always my favourite, because no matter what I do, I always have the next day to recuperate being the day of rest, the Sabbath day. It is for me a day of rest and I had in mind to continue what I started with Danielle, meaning, instruct her about Jesus' messages. I don't know exactly why, but that makes me particularly happy to do it even if the person I'm talking to is not too receptive.

"Hi you, how are you doing tonight?" "I'm very well James, and you?" "Me too Danielle since I have a day off tomorrow finally. We can make love all night if we want to. We have all day tomorrow to get back on our feet. Do you have any news from Janene?" "Not much, it was bad reception on the phone. She'll be here on Sunday. If you don't mind we'll go take a bath and then go to bed, I got a surprise for you." "Now you got me curious, what is it?" "Well, you'll see." "Ho, come on shoot. Don't be cruel by keeping me on a hook." "You got to wait James, its something I have to show you." "And you can't tell me what it is?" "You know that patient is a virtue." "I'm not too sure to be very virtual, you know?" "I won't tell you anyway, I'll show you later." "Let's hurry then." "James, we have all night for ourselves." "You're right, I'm sorry, but I'm still curious." "I'm pretty sure that you're going to like it." "Let me soap you all over, would you?" "I was wondering what you were waiting for." "I was kind of distracted by an intriguing woman who likes suspense.

You like this?" "I love it." "Good, because it's a job I like to do." "Ho, that's a job now." "I hope I'm doing it right?" "You're too good, I'm about to come." "Let yourself go, we have all night. Hooooooooooooooo, too late, you got me."

She held me real tight for a long time and I understood that she appreciated it.

"Let's dry ourselves and go to bed, ok?" "Hold me tight, my legs are weak." "Don't worry, I can carry you if you want?" "I don't think it will be necessary, although it could be fun."

"And up we go, we're going to bed pretty princess with your prince." "Yes M Prince! Wow, you're not very big, but strong like Hercules." "You're as light as a feather." "One hundred and twenty pounds, a feather?" "Well, maybe two!" "Ha, ha, ha, very funny." "Lift up the blankets, would you?" "Here we are." "Down we go, let me taste this thing now." "No James, it's my turn to give you pleasure. Lie on your back and let me do it, alright?" "Mmmmm, I'm welling to, but I'm not used to it." "You'll get used to it, believe me." "I don't mind trying. Mmmmmm, mmmmm it's good, so good. Watchhhhhhh. What did you do? Everything suddenly blocked." "It works. Let me do it again if you like it." "If I like it? But it's superbly good." "Now you taste a bit salty, a little bit like oysters." "I hope you like them, because it's so gooddddd. Watchhhhhhhh! Everything blocked again." "It works good." "But what are you doing?" "I just follow the psychologist instructions and it works." "It's a nice job." "It's a real pleasure." "All the pleasure is for me." "You're wrong, I got really excited doing this." "So, that is the surprise you had for me?" "That's it." "Now I know why you didn't want to tell me." "Do you want some more?" "As much as you want to give me sweetheart. Mmmmm! Mmmmm, it's so good. Mmmmm! Watch! Mmmmm! Watch! Your trick is good, I managed to hold back twice." "Now I'm all excited." "Ho yea, I'll fix that for you pretty princess, you'll see."

I managed to make love to her for at least thirty minutes and I could hold back the ejaculation as I wanted to, which I could never do before. She counted four orgasms and I stopped only because she wanted to. It's was only then I let myself go. I never experienced such a pleasure in my whole life. The pleasure to give pleasure to the one you love is tremendous. I cannot say any better, it's tremendous.

"I never though it could be that good James." "Me neither!" "Wait till Janene hear about this." "Please don't tell her anything, we'll get her the surprise." "She won't believe her own ass." "You're quite funny too, when you want to. Tell me, what did the psychologist tell you?" "She said; you could do it yourselves or you could do it with your partner. The guy can masturbate himself or she can masturbate him and when he's ready to ejaculate you strangle the penis right under the head that will block the flow and after a few good practices the guy learns to do it automatically. I can tell that you learn quickly, because you succeeded on the first time." "Ho, I'm sure we're going to need a few more practices just to make it perfect." "You enjoyed that, didn't you?" "I just loved it." "I wonder why so many women don't want to hear about oral sex, it did excite me so much, I was ready to come even before you touch me." "We're going to have to find a way for you to hold back too." "Very funny!" "Apparently half of men love it a lot like I do and the other half simply hates it. I wonder if it's because they don't really like women or if it's because half of the women are not eatable." "What do you mean by that? Not eatable!" "Well, I mean that they don't all taste good, some women are sweet like you and Janene and others are rather sour. For myself if you were sour even though I love you very much I know

I couldn't. I would just bring up. It would be real sad, but I won't be able to. It could make two people very sad." "So, Janene and I are really lucky?" "I think the three of us are really lucky. Well all this is appetizing. Aren't you hungry?" "Do you want to eat me?" "A little bit later if you don't mind, right now I'd like a few toasts and a cup of tea." "I just hope I'll have the strength to get up." "I can help you if you like or I can carry you one more time?" "That's alright, I'll be fine, thank you." "It's already pass four, we'll have to sleep a bit." "I thought I heard you say that we have all night?" "You can talk, you can hardly get up to make a few toasts." "I really feel weak and I didn't even have a drink." "And look how young you are." "Don't forget, it's only my second time." "Ho right, I forgot, excuse me?"

We took a little snack and then we both went back to bed and we woke up to the sound of the phone at one in afternoon. Danielle answered it to hear the sweet voice of Janene.

"Allô, Danielle here." "It's me, how are you?" "I'm very well."

"James it's Janene." "Let me talk to her, would you?" "Here ! "

"How things on your side?" "There is still a lot of snow as usual to the height of the roof." "It was not the best time of the year to go in this part of the country, that's for sure." "It takes what it takes. The storm is out of the house too. I got to tell you that I understood your parable just in time." "I'm glad, because that means you will understand all the others too." "What is that mean? Is that another parable?" "No, but Danielle will talk to you about it when you're back. It's nothing really, don't worry. Alright, I'll let you talk to Danielle now. See you soon, I love you." "Me too !"

"Allô ! Danielle, I will arrive at the station at four tomorrow." "I will come to get you, but don't forget your cell phone."

"I will come too Danielle."

"James will come with me Janene." "That's wonderful. Alright then, I'll see you tomorrow." "See you, I can't wait."

"While I'm on the phone I'll call my parents." "That's good I got to go to the washroom anyway."

"Ring ring, ring ring." "Allô !" "Is that you dad?" "Danielle, my sweetheart, it's been a long time since we heard from you. How are you?"

"Joanne, it's Danielle, pick up the other phone."

"I am marvellously good daddy. I met a very fine young man and I'm just crazy about him." "Wow, for a news that a big one coming from you. Usually you're not so quick when it comes to men." "That's because this one is rather special." "What is he doing for a living?" "He's a houses builder, a contractor." "It's a good trade and it's good everywhere." "But dad, I call you for an all different and a particular reason." "Ho yea ! What is it?" "Do you still have your bible?" "Ho my God, it's been a long time since I took it. I let father st Germain read it to us every Sunday." "You've already answered one of my questions." "Give me a minute or two and I'll go get it."

"Hi mom ! How are you? I'm fine Danielle, but I have to tell you to take your time with your new boyfriend. Some times it takes a long time to get to know a person, you know?" "Not this one mom! This one you know him when you meet him."

"I'm here Danielle with the bible in my hands. What do you want to know?" "Do you want to open it at Matthew 23, verse 9?" "Give me a second there. Sweetie, we cannot talk about those things." "Why not dad? Should we destroy the truth or simply hide it?" "You, you've been talking with a Jehovah witness, haven't you?" "Not at all dad, but I talked to someone who seems to know about the truth. Do you have a piece of paper and a pen? It will be good for you to take a few notes." "Yes, I got that here near by. Go read Exodus 20, it's the law of God and take a special look at the verses 8 – 11 and then go read Matthew 5, verses 17 and 18. Be really careful when you read this, would you?" "You know that we were worn that we could go crazy by reading the bible." "Was that said by a psychologist or by a priest?" "It was a priest of course. But you have to be careful to whom you talk to sweetie. There are trouble makers out there. All this can drive a person crazy, you know?" "Well, it's true that it is disturbing to find out we've been lied to for years, specially by those who condemned us to hell for lying. If leaving the religion because I was lied to is crazy, so be it, I'm crazy too. Jesus told us that it was better to lose one hand than to burn in hell maybe it's better to lose my mind too. Do you believe in Jesus-Christ dad?" "Of course, I believe in him." "Do you believe more in your religion than in Jesus?" "The church is infallible Danielle." "I believe that the church has infallibly lied to people and the proof is right there in the bible. I'm sorry, but I will take the word of Jesus and the word of God before the word of any other one. If you believe in Jesus go read Matthew 24, 15 where it said; "May the reader be careful when he reads. Seek and you shall find." Jesus said in Matthew 7, 7 and because I love you so very much I want you to look for and to find the truth that the church has hidden from us." "But you've become a real priest Danielle." "Don't insult me dad, I love the truth." "Well, I didn't want to insult you sweetheart, I just think that you are a good preacher, that's all." "I'm going to let you go now. It's not too cold up there in the North?" "We had worst, believe me. Take good care of yourself sweetie." "You too, I love you both. Bye!" "Bye sweetie !"

"Did you fall asleep in there James?" "No, I was just resting while waiting for you." "It's true, it's the Sabbath day." "You should come and join me, it's nice in the water." "Do you think it's wrong for us to sleep together?" "Well, it depends." "It depends on what?" "If you sleep with me because you love me and you want to be my wife, then you have not sin. You simply became my wife. Go read how Rebekah became Isaac's wife in Genesis 24, 67. I'll do it as soon as we get out of the tub." "It's the same way Joseph, father of Jesus took Mary for his wife." "What do you think about priests, friars and nuns who don't get married?" "I think that if they don't get married to please God, they have made an enormous mistake." "Really?" "After God created man, He created a woman, saying it was not good for a man to be alone. That is still true today. He told them to be fruitful, to multiply and to fill up the earth. I don't think that God is for abortion and neither for celibate. It takes a man and a woman to multiply. God made us to his image, meaning creators. That is the reason why he made sex so enjoyable. Some priests condemned my mother to hell for avoiding pregnancy after having thirteen kids and all of them avoid multiplying by not getting married. For her last one it was almost suicide or attempt murder and she was even pronounced dead at her delivery, but God by miracle brought her back to life. The baby only lived twenty-three hours. My mom's mother died with two twins in her belly, because her priest told her that she has to do her duty. A nurse kept her warm until the doctor arrived to give her a caesarean. One baby girl lived a whole fifteen minutes and the other girls a whole twenty minutes. Her doctor told her that she couldn't have anymore because of the asthma she was plagued with. My dad's mother died of similar reasons. The results were that my parents have hardly known their mothers and I never had the chance to know my grand mothers. Today doctors decide without consulting priests or pastors what is slowing down the killing of so many women and children. Now when you read John 8, 44, it is written; "He was a murderer from the beginning, he is a liar and the father of lies." "Does that remind you of anybody?" "The church, the religions!" "Let me tell you that you're on your way to become a great disciple. Maybe we should get out of the tub now, the water is getting cold." "How do you do it? I could listen to you for hours." "That is only because you love the word of God too." "But you know all those verses by heart." "I love the word of God too." "But, how come you know all these things? How come you know so much?" "It's simple, I follow Jesus of Nazareth, the one who was crucified, I follow the God of Israel, the one who created everything. Now if you translate this in French you will read; I am Jesus of Nazareth and I am the God of Israel. I mean in French I am and I follow translate the same way (Je suis)." "But you don't mean to say that you are God." "I would never say such a thing, although according to what Jesus said and what Christianity teaches, I am God's brother." "You are God's brother? Ho, come on now James, that is beyond understanding. You don't think it is a bit pretentious?" "Not at all sweetie, it is only the truth according to the bible." "I never heard such a thing." "You never heard the church teach that Jesus is a man made God." "That I heard, yes." "Now if Jesus is God and the same Jesus surely didn't lie when he said that the one who does the will of his Father in heaven, this one is his brother, his sister and his mother. You can read it in Matthew 12, 50." "Let me see that. But you are absolutely right. If Jesus is God and the one who does the will of his Father, what you're doing, is his brother, then you are God's brother." "Exactly!" "People will say that you are crazy to say such a thing even though it's true.

I can also tell you that I heal people and I resurrect them too." "That must be another one of your traps?" "There are no traps like you said and remember that I love the truth." "But I cannot follow you dear." "That will come. Go read Ezekiel 18 completely and you will find out two things very important, first that we are not accountable for the sins of our parents and neither of our first parents (Adam and Eve, the original sin) like the Christian church made us responsible for and that we are not responsible for the sins of our children either. Jesus healed the sinners by teaching the word of God and he resurrected them by leading them to God and away from religion. That's what he did then and continue to do today. The medicine is the Word of God. That is also what I'm doing with you." "It's true that I have a lot to learn and I don't know much about God, but because of you, all this is changing now." "We're having a good start. It's five, are you making supper?" "I don't work on Sabbath day anymore if I can do otherwise and I don't really feel like cooking." "The Sabbath will be over in one hour, but if you like I can take you to your favourite restaurant." "Ho, that would be so sweet." "Let's go and later on we can maybe go dancing for a bit." "That would be sweeter yet." "Let's get dressed and get some fresh air."

So we went for supper and talked about all kind of things. After supper we walked until the time of the dance arrived. We danced and we danced until we were out of breath. That day was for Danielle and I another one of a long journey of complete happiness. A couple of weeks later her father called and mentioned that he began to have doubts about the religion and the teaching of the church. The good seed was planted in good soil. The next day Janene came back from her trip very happy to get back with us. Danielle who loves the word of God as much as I do didn't waste any time to start teaching Janene. Janene understood very quickly what I meant when I mentioned another parable. There is something else she understood very quickly.

"You must have met with the psychologist, because since I came back from my parents you make me come like never before?" "I didn't, but I learn to listen to her anyway." "How did you get the information?" "Danielle got it for me and gave it to me in a very special way. The important thing is that it works."

We live very happy every day for many months and one day Danielle noticed a change in her hormonal system.

"James, I need to talk to you about something very important." "Alright, what is the problem my love?" "I don't want you to feel obligated in any way, shape or form, but you're going to be a father in seven months. Well, this is a wonderful news sweetie. Did you tell Janene too?" "Not yet, you're the first one to know it beside my gynaecologist." "How could you ever hide this from your very best friend?" "I just found out about it myself. I think that it's also time to talk about having a house built, because I don't want to raise our child in an apartment. I want him to have a place to run and to play." "You're absolutely right, but this conversation concern Janene too, you know?" "Of course it is, but I wanted to know your reaction first." "Danielle, my love, I'm ready for this day since the first time I laid my eyes on you. You must have noticed that I never took any protection to go with you." "I thought that you just relied on me to avoid pregnancy." "I mainly relied on you to decide when you want to start a family but, I've been ready since the beginning." "I love you so much, I always knew that you were the man that

I needed." "You mean that you both needed. That's what I was saying." "When can we continue this conversation between the three of us?" "Next week we both work day time, we'll have all the evenings to discuss everything." "That is wonderful and tell me, did you do it on purpose?" "What do you mean?" "To get pregnant, did you do it on purpose?" "Let just say that I was ready for it and I wasn't careful anymore." "I was under the impression that you were looking for me a little more often lately. That is going to bring some major changes in our lives, you're realizing that don't you?"

"You said you're ready and I have been too for quite a while so, there is no problem." "There is one anyway." "What is it?" "I don't want the baby to be an illegitimate child, a state child, we got to get married." "I just don't want you to feel obligated, you know?" "I don't feel obligated at all, but you see, all of my parents' children were called and treated like bastards in the village where we grew up and I don't want that to happen to my children." "Why? Weren't they married?" "They were married alright, but it was just like they weren't." "I really don't understand. Well you see, the priest of the village as usual called for my parents' birth certificates from where they were from and from where they were baptized and all that, but when he received them, it was not mentioned that they were married. The stupid man didn't bother talking to my parents about it either. My parent's witnesses were still alive fortunately, but for us kids, the wrong was done." "What happened to you?" "We were jeered for almost the entire school time." "That is terrible and so unfair." "What can you do, the church is infallible." "Poor you, you kids had an unhappy childhood." "Yes, but I'm happy about it now." "How can you be happy now for having been unhappy when you were young?" "Because, that lead me to look for and to find the truth that I know today and I can share it with you and with all the people that I meet. Believe me, there is no greater feeling. I am free like the wind, free from any slavery. Even if you were the only one who listens to me, it would be worth it." "You're an incredible good soul person my man, you know?" "If you say it I want to believe it." "What else can you tell me today about the lies and contradictions that you found." "There are big one and obvious ones. Take John 3, 16. It is written that God so loved the world. Well He so loved the world that He asked his people to retrieve from it, that the world is the way of perdition. It is written that He sacrificed his one and only son, which would mean that Jesus is his first born. Now we can read in Luke 3, 38 that Adam who was born four thousands years earlier was also the son of God and would also be his first born. Now it is written that Jesus is the only son of God when it is also written that Adam is the son of God. Somebody somewhere lied. It is written in Genesis 6, 2 "That the sons of God saw that the daughters of men were pretty and they took them for wives among the ones they chose. Now that means the angels were also sons of God and they obviously like sex too. Now if you go to Deuteronomy 32, 19, and read; "The Lord Almighty was angered with his sons and daughters." What is surprising me truly and the most Danielle is the fact that I never heard anybody talked about this before. Think about all the teachers the searchers, the pastors, the scholars, the preachers, the priests, the bishops, and the infallible popes and more who are and were on earth. The bible is the most sold book in the world, for what I heard, is it possible that so many billions of peoples were blinded that much." "Maybe it's because the time wasn't yet come or worst yet and that scares me a bit, maybe everyone who talked about it were killed like Jesus." "You got a point there. It's not at all impossible, because Jesus predicted that. Now remember I read the sons of God, the angels took the women on earth." "Yes, why?" "Well, God was so mad about it that He almost destroyed the whole earth with the flood and almost all the people who were on it." "Yes, but that seems to me quite fair." "Who do you think the sons of God were then?" "I would think that they were bad angels." "That's what I think too. But I still don't see where the problem is." "You see, God condemned and almost destroyed the world and its people because of the bad angels who slept with women and bare children to them and He would have done the same thing with Mary, the mother of Jesus. It is an absolute abomination in a holy place (the bible) that Jesus talked about in Matthew 24, 15. The end is near by, believe me. Jesus to be the Messiah has to be fathered by one of King David descendant and not by a Holy Spirit that was not yet in the world according to many verses in the bible, in John's gospel. See The Acts 2, 2-13. My God, James, that means we are at the end of ages." "That is why we have to make disciples of all nations and teach them everything that Jesus has commanded. Look in Matthew 28, 20." "That is a lot of dough."

"Yes, I hope to be able to multiply the bread like Jesus did." "You have already started James." "I'm going to start a chain letter coming from a Jesus' disciple and sent it around the world to wake up a few people who will read it, hoping that they too multiply the bread of life." "Well, that's enough for me today." "One more question if you allow me." "What do you have in mind?" "The baby and baptism!" "You're asking me what I think of it?" "Yes ! Jesus was circumcised at eight days old and he was baptized when he was thirty years old. I think that we have to believe in God and know about Him before we can get baptized. There are a lot of babies who were baptized and turned out to be real devils. Jesus said that the children already belong to the kingdom of heaven and nobody can answer for others. John the Baptist said that he baptized with water, but Jesus who is more powerful will baptize with fire and with the Holy Ghost and the two did it to bring people to repentance. You can see that in Matthew 3, 11. So we agree that the baby will be baptized if and when he decides for himself. Right now you are being baptized with the Holy Ghost, the word of God." "That is a lot of stuff." "You do good to stop me when you have enough. You know that I'm in it for the rest of my life. Good

night my sweetheart." "Good night my man."

A few days later we had this famous discussion about the new life that was ahead of us. Even though the child was very welcome he was going to change a lot of things in our habits.

"We're going to need a big house." "Yes Janene and I think we should build it in the country to avoid gossips and tittle-tattles of the town. It's going to be a lot of talks as soon as somebody sees me kissing one and the other of you two." "Janene and I don't give a shit about what will people say." "You will change your mind when they attack the children." "I didn't think about that aspect." "What do you suggest? " "I think we should be looking for a big acreage or even better a nice farm around here not to far from town. To tell you the truth, I would like to raise a few animals beside the children of course." "We didn't know that side of you." "Well Danielle, you should know by now that I am full of surprises. I hope it's not too disappointing." "Not at all, in fact, I think that you have very good ideas."

"What do you think Janene?" "I think we have a man who amazes me more and more." "Me too! So what are we doing?"

"We look for a little farm even if there is nothing on it." "I agree." "We could build one or two or even three houses according to our taste and resources." "We could also build a duplex where everyone could have is own quarters. You could travel from one flat to the other instead than one room to the other." "Can I make another suggestion?" "Of course you can, you are the corner stone of our life." "I suggest that we build a triplex where each one of you would have her flat attached to mine situated in the middle of you two. One would be on the right and the other one on the left. It will be a picture of us three." "What a marvellous idea!" "Myself, I want three large bedrooms, a large bathroom, and another one medium size, a large kitchen and a large dining room."

"That will be good for me too. I can build the size that you want. That is going to be a castle. We can only afford it if we build in the country." "You're right, I vote for this."

"Me too!" "Then we all agree. It's going to be expansive." "Do you have any idea?" "It's going to be between four and fife hundreds thousands dollars if I build it." "Our condo is almost paid for and worth a bit better than two hundreds thousands and we both have a little more than one hundred thousand each at the bank." "My house is all paid for and I presently have an offer of one hundred and eighty thousands, besides, the guy is getting impatient. So this means that money is not an issue." "How much time do you need to complete the work?" "From five to six months, but I have to finish all the contracts in course first." "How long will that take?" "I'm pretty sure it will take between thirty and forty-five days. That is if I postpone one house that is not too much in a hurry." "That means our house could be ready for the coming of our first born." "Chances are real good." "Ho, that would be so great." "Don't choke me Danielle, like you say, it is a lot of dough. Multiply darling, multiply, we need it." "In the mean time we have a marriage to attempt. Would you have time to take care of the preparations Danielle?" "Yes, Janene will help me and I don't see any problem for now."

"Talking about multiplications, I'm getting old and you can't put me on hold, because I want four children at the very least." "Are you sure that three bedrooms will be enough Janene? We'll set two girls in one room, two boys in another and papa and mama in the third one, it should be ok. We could always finish the basement later." "Then everything is fine. With the two of you and all my work, I'll be very busy. Can you also keep an eye on properties for sale? Maybe we should put an ad in the papers specifying what we're looking for. If we buy a farm that nobody wants, it will be cheap. All is really matter for us is that it is not too far from town, from your work. That reminds me that I have a hard day work tomorrow, I should go to bed. It's your turn tonight Janene, don't wait too long if you want your candy." "If I miss you tonight, I'll catch you in the morning." "As you wish. Come on give me a hug before I disappear in the dreams of the night."

I thought that they needed to talk between themselves and I didn't want to be in their way for that. Besides, a night without sex was almost welcome for me. At this stage of our lives our families had so, so accepted our living situation. One thing was still bothering me and that was the question of polygamy. I knew for sure that both wanted to marry me. We had to find a solution to this problem and that was coming pretty urgent. So I got on the internet churching for some answers. On the Mormon side I found a lot of answers on Christianity and gospels, but nothing at all on marriages as if that was taboo. I think I will have to go meet one of their ministers in person to get some answers from that side. The unique idea of been obligated to be part of a religion no matter which one makes me sick to my stomach. There is one thing that Jesus said and I cannot forget in Mathew 6, 24; "No man can serve two masters; for either he will hate the one and love the other; or else he will hold to the one, and despise the other. You cannot serve God and Mammon." I'll have to find a different way. As far as I am concern, deep inside of me, I am already married to each one of them as much as Salomon was married to his seven hundreds wives or King David who walk according to the heart of God.

"So you're going to get married before me." "James is insisting that we get married before the baby is born." "It would be wonderful if we could get married the same day. I don't think that there will be an easy way. What ever happens Janene, you will never be left behind. I don't think it is a question of heart for James, but rather a question of legality. He loves you just as much as he loves me if not more." "Poor guy, it must not be too easy for him all the time. I trust him, he seems to always find a way to do things. Did you think about how many kids you want?" "Not really, I just want to take this one at the time. It's wonderful the way he plans to install us in a sort of castle away from mean people and evil eyes and ears." "I think too that it's going to be wonderful to live on a small farm that we own. It's going to be just wonderful for the kids too and they'll have everything to be happy. Are you serious when you say you want four children?" "Can't be more serious than that." "Between the two of us we could have a dozen kids. It takes the two of us to equal his mother." "Can you imagine thirteen kids, the same woman." "No! That's not for me. Doesn't it scare you a bit too all the knowledge he's got on the bible?" "A little bit, I have to admit, knowing that not that long ago, people like him were accused of witchcraft and were burnt alive. Luckily it's not like this anymore." "I'm not so sure about that." "Stop right there, you're scaring me." "There are murders in the world that we'll never know how it happened and neither why. Louis Riel is one of them and all we know is how he died, but why, it is still a question mark in the mind of a lot of people. They sure got rid of him. He must have known something that they didn't want him to talk about. His wife became a very young widow and his kids were young orphans. How did he died and why?" "They accused him of treason, but James things that he too had a lot of knowledge about the truth and he made the mistake to talk with his friend, a bishop about it. James things that he might have been a trader to his religion when he found the truth, but not a trader to the country. The judge asked him if he had a last wish before the sentence and he said; "My wish your honour would be that we separate from Rome for it is the cause of divisions in the world." The six juries were Christians and so was the judge. That was enough to declare him guilty. That was the end of the poor man, he was hanged and the truth was choked with him for another hundred years or so." "But that means James' life only hold by one tread." "Don't be scare, everyone's life is hold by one tread, yours and mine too, but at least his is worth living. He has a physical and spiritual strength that is out of the ordinary and he will know how to spread the truth safely. He did it so far." "That is true and because of him we are not as ignorant as we used to be. What ever it is, we should go to bed now." "It is not two o'clock, is it?" "Yes dear, it is very late." "We only have five hours left to sleep. We should set up two alarm clocks. Good night!" "Good night, sleep well."

"Janene, Janene, it's time to get up, you're working this morning." "Whatttttttttt? I want to sleep."

"It's almost seven, you got to go to work. You stayed up late, didn't you? I got to go now, have a good day." "Byeeeeeeeeeeee!"

"Danielle, I got to go and leave you handle Janene, she's got a hard time to get up. Have a good day." "You too my love."

Chapter 3

I went directly home and I phoned the foreman to delegate enough work for the day. Then I took my breakfast and after that I sat at my drawing table to put on paper what I had in mind. It was not too easy to concentrate on this important work, because the phone wouldn't stop ringing. Three of them were potential customers who insisted that my company build their houses. The only problem was the timing, because I was not available before August, unless I hire more staff. Staff that you cannot keep an eye on constantly could be very dangerous. I already lost a lot of money with subcontractors who didn't really care about the job well done or not. Those are life's lessons that you don't want to forget too easily. It's better to make a little less money than to lose some. Do, undo and redo are expensive matters. After all it's better to do later what you cannot do now. Who has ears to hear can hear! Despite everything happened at the end of the day I had quite a bit done. The main drawing was done, but there was quite a bit to do to complete the plan. Of course I had still a lot to discuss with my two adorable women, but I was sure it would only be insignificant details like the color of the walls and the cupboards. I was done with all the calculations as far as what that famous house will cost, but I decided not to talk about it until I have everything on hand. I learned the hard way that it was best not to talk to your customers about prices until you can show them what they're getting for their money. Ho sure, my customers this time were my own wives, but nevertheless, it was their money that was involve in this project too. They both wanted something big, I think they going to have something grandiose. The size of that house will be 5472 square feet, beside the garage underneath and the two basements. I built a seven suites building once that was a lot smaller than this house. What ever my ladies want, I want it too. We still had to find a piece of land to build it on. At five to five the phone rang again, but this time it was the wonderful voice of the mom to be.

"Is that you James?" "Is that me that you want to talk to, my angel?" "Nobody else! Supper is ready and the table is set, we are waiting for you and you cannot refuse." "I need a bit of time to wash and shave and I'll be right there." "Don't take too long, it's good when it's hot." "I'll be there within a half hour." "See you soon, I love you." "I love you too."

I rush to the bathroom, because I didn't want to let these two wonderful women in waiting for they don't have that many occasions to reunite all three of us that often for supper and talk. They often have to take turns at nights and evenings at the hospital. Thirty five minutes later I sat down with them at their table. I had anticipated an evening of discussions about the house and maybe where we could build it and all that, but it was completely different. I couldn't believe it when I heard;

"Happy birthday to you, happy birthday to you, happy birthday dear James, happy birthday to you."

There were about twenty guesses hiding in the bedrooms that came out at the moment the desert was served. My mother and a few of my sisters were some of the guesses who answered the invitation. Danielle's parents, some of their friends and some co-workers were also invited to the party. I'm not too crazy about that kind of surprise parties, but nevertheless, this one was important for what was coming down the road. I was very happy to finally meet Danielle's parents. They sure had a lot to say about the catholic religion and they had a lot of questions about the lies in contradictions that could be found in the holy bible. They were asking endless questions and I had to be almost rude to get away and introduce them both to my mother. I wanted to get near Danielle who herself had a bit of a problem to get away from the young doctor. Janene seemed to have a good time with my sisters who wanted to know how she was coping in our three ways relationship. I was really concerned about the young doctor strange behaviour. He was the type of men who likes to blame and to lecture others. So I invited Danielle to follow me to a bedroom for a few minutes.

"Danielle, is there a problem with your doctor friend?" "He never acted like this before." "Do you know what his problem is?" "I'm under the impression that he knows about Janene and I with you." "But even if he knew it all, that's not of his business at all." "Are you sure there is nothing else?" "I think that he is a bit jealous and he would like to be in your shoes. My shoes are way too small for him, but this is not the problem, he seemed to be pestering you for the last half hour." "He has a position to cause me a lot of trouble at work." "You're not going to give to black mailing, are you?" "It is not my intention, but anyway I love my work." "I don't think you should jeopardize your happiness for your work." "Don't worry, I love you and you'll always be my priority." "I knew it, but it's always nice to hear it. Do you want me to talk to him?" "No, I will just tell him what I just told you and if he doesn't get it, then you'll talk to him yourself. Are you alright with that?" "It is as you wish sweetie, but as far as I am concerned, he's not welcome to my party. I'll be happier if you ask him to leave." "I'll do it and forgive me for inviting him." "It's not your fault if he is an idiot. We should go before they all wonder if we are making love." "Frankly, it wouldn't be that bad of an idea."

We got out of the room to everyone wondering eyes, but the doctor had already excused himself and left. I think he sensed the hot water and guessed what was going on. I just knew then that this was a story to be followed. I knew too that I'll have to clear things up with my two lovers. The party had started early and had to be over early, because almost everyone was working the next day. At ten all the guesses were gone and we had to pick up all the glasses and dishes that went to the dishwasher. All the empty bottles and cans went in the boxes that I'll have to take to a bottles depot.

"No point asking you if you liked your party, darling." "It was a surprise party with a few surprises, but my birthday is only next week." "We have something else organized for next week and that is why we choose tonight where we could bring in a few peoples." "I thought your parents were very nice, interesting and interested." "They love the truth just like me and that makes me very happy."

"I wish I could say the same thing about mine." "Maybe that will come some day Janene, but one has to love God and his word more than himself and mainly more than his religion." "Tell me Danielle, what the heck happened with Raymond?" "I kind of understood that he wanted to make me understand something about you Janene as if he wanted to cause trouble between us." "I know what his problem is." "Tell us, what it is?" "Last year he was after me and I think that he is after you now. He thinks that James is cheating on you with me. I made him understand that I wasn't interested in him at all and I think you should do the same if you're not interested in him." "Me, be interested in him, I rather die. Neither him or anybody else, I have the man that I want."

"Tell me Danielle why did you invite him exactly?" "Well, he was quite gentle and he basically invited himself. I know that he doesn't have that many friends and I gave in. I'm going to put him in his place as soon as tomorrow." "Good, that's enough talking about him. What would you say if we go to bed now? Who's turn?" "It's still mine, but Danielle needs you more than I do tonight. She's sad and she needs to be taking care of. I had a very good time with your sisters James. They were very curious to know how you could satisfy both of us and they found it very strange that there was no jealousy between Danielle and I. I think I convinced them at least that's the impression I got." "You're wonderful. I love you and good night."

"Good night Danielle and take advantage of it." "I will put all my heart to it as you would yourself. Thanks!" "You're welcome, but not too often."

"Don't worry Janene you will lose nothing by waiting." "Sleep well on Thursday, because I'll keep you up all night on Friday." "It's promising."

After a bit of cleaning up, we all went to bed. I watched Janene pull away with a bit of nostalgia I have to admit, but I also knew that I was not losing anything by getting in bed with Danielle.

"You're not too mad at me?" "Neither one of us have anything to blame you for my love and who knows, the future will tell, it might be one of the best thing you ever done. I mean, inviting him. I don't understand, but if you say so, it's got to be true." "Now, enough talking about all this, keep quiet and let me love you my way, alright? And try not to scream too loud, Janene needs some sleep. When I scream it's because it's so good I think I'm going to die. I want to make love to you so much I want you to be touch. I'm telling you with no lie make love to you till you die. I put those words in a song one day." "I'd like you to sing it to me sometimes." "Not now, right now I'm hungry." "Help yourself, the meal is ready." "Hum, the fruit is juicy and delicious."

I made love to her until the middle of the night hoping that the walls of this building have not too many ears and that Janene had ear plugs. Both Danielle and I had a hard time getting up that morning. It's not easy for me to stay in good mood all day in those days, but when I seemed to lose patient, I only have to think at what kept me awake and everything is alright again.

Danielle didn't waste any time confronting Raymond, the young doctor, who is almost always on the same shift than her at work.

"Raymond, when you'll have a minute I need to talk to you." "I have time now, let's go to the conferences room. You look gorgeous this morning, what did you have for breakfast?" "The same thing as usual, but I made love almost all night with James and I'm pregnant with him, that might be the reason I look like blooming. Can you tell me what was your problem last night? Do you realize that you spoiled our evening? I didn't appreciate it at all." "I'm sorry, but it wasn't my intention." "Tell me what your intention was exactly?" "Are you sure that your James is completely honest with you? " "There is no man on earth who is as honest as he is. I don't mean to hurt you, but let me tell you one thing, you can't hold a candle to him." "That is yet to be proven." "For you maybe, but to me it's all settled." "I think he's cheating on you with Janene. One thing is sure, Janene is crazy about him and it's obvious to everyone." "Who could blame her? He is a wonderful man and handsome above all." "It doesn't bother you that he could be cheating on you with your best friend?" "Janene is the most faithful friend I could get. She's a friend that one could say; always and forever." "If it's the way you see things, I have nothing more to say." "I sure hope you won't say anymore on that matter, do you understand me?" "This is clear enough, thank you." "That's all I had to say, good day."

She went out of the room leaving him thinking behind her, but yet she wasn't convinced that this was enough for him to get rid of his obsession. On my side after checking on my jobs and see that the work was going on normally, I went back to my drawing table to work on my dream house that got me more and more excited. I was also dying to let my girls know about it.

Only one thing worried me a little, the cost was going to be higher than previously estimated. They both saw big and I designed big. The total link of that house will be one hundred and fifty-two feet. Such a house in the city would cost at least twenty thousands dollars in taxes alone a year. At three thirty in the afternoon I called at the condo to let them know that I will be having supper with my mom and that I will come to see them at around nine that evening. Mom still thinks that we're wrong to live like we do.

"Are you conscious that you're going to have the whole society against you?" "This is not true mom, there are communities in Canada where men have more than one wife and many children." "It is still not accepted very well." "All it matters to me is that I'm in good terms with God." "God gave Adam only one woman and she was named Eve." "Well God couldn't have been boning Adam completely just after making him to give him more wives. Some day we'll know how many wives Adam and Jesus had." "Jesus didn't have a wife." "I'm not so sure." "What make you say such a thing?" "First in John 3, 2 a Pharisee, man of the Law came to Jesus and called him Rabbi. I just happen to know that to be a Rabbi a man had to be thirty years old, have ten followers and he has to be married." "That is beyond me." "You also know that there were many women who followed and served him. Did he need that many women to serve him, he who didn't even have a home? Besides, they discovered Jesus tomb lately and the name of Mary Magdalene is inscribed on it. For that to happen, she had to be either his sister or his wife." "That is only a supposition for now." "Maybe so, the truth will come out sooner or later. There is another very important thing I have to tell you mom and that is Jesus had in heart to do the will of God, the Father Who is in heaven. One of the first will of God for men is to be fruitful, to multiply and to fill up the earth." "It was also said that each man has his wife." "That is yet better than to say; if you don't marry you do better. Or yet to say like Paul: "I wish that all men were like me." No wife and no children! We'll have to talk about this another time mom, I told the girls that I would be there by nine, that doesn't leave me much time to get there."

What surprises me the most in the conversations with almost everybody, including my mom is the fact that they swallowed the lies with mouth full, they have digested them with no problem and I have to give them the truth in very small amount, with a little spoon and yet that with a lot of precautions. It's true though that the truth is a medicine to their sickness. There was a good reason for Jesus to say in Matthew 10, 8;" "Heal the sick." "It is also true that a sick person who knows is sick is not as sick as a person who is sick and doesn't know it. It was already nine fifteen when I got at the apartment's door step. My two charming women were waiting impatiently. For Danielle it was to tell me about her conversation with the young doctor and for Janene it was to tell me about the four properties she had found that could be very interesting for us.

"I think that Raymond got the message now. You should have seen his face when I told him that we made love almost all night and that I was pregnant with you." "He didn't suggest abortion, I hope?" "No, but I'm sure it is not because he didn't want to." "I think he will leave us alone from now on." "Let's hope so."

"Janene, you seem anxious to tell me something. Do you have some good news?" "Yes, since we talked about it, I'm dying to know where we're going to live and where we going to have this dream house built." "Well, I'm almost done with the blue prints and I'm pretty sure you're going to like it. I spent almost the whole week working on them. You really have our happiness at heart, don't you?" "My sweethearts, it's the only thing that matters." "What a charming man you are. It's my turn tonight, but you're not going to make love to me." "Did I do something wrong?" "On the contrary, but I'll make love to you. You'll get the full treatment." "That's promising, I can hardly wait."

"Would you stop the two of you, I'm going to come just by listening to both of you."

"I'm sorry Danielle, that was not my goal." "I know it, but it's just like watching a sexual movie with my favourite actor."

"You're not going to play with yourself, are you?" "I rather wait than to feel too lonely."

"That's enough, let's get back to business." "I found two different five acres pieces of land, one old abandoned farm on which run a little river. There are also a ruin house and a ruin barn just good for firewood." "Do you know how far this one is from town?" "Just a minute, I got that here. It is at eighteen kilometres from the town's limit." "Is that too far for the two of you " "Not for me!"

"Not for me either, besides, we can travel with you many times." "I would travel farther than that to reach the dream house." "There is a big problem though." "What is it?" "There are a lot of scrubs growing back and more than half of the property is forest like." "Maybe we can turn that to our advantage. Do you know in which zone is it?" "Yes, it is in an agricultural farm zone and I was told that it will most likely never change." "That is good news." "What do you mean?" "That means it will never be anybody too close to us." "That's true too, we could be like in paradise." "This way we could at least choose our neighbours." "We could also make a little beach with the river." "That is not so sure." "Why?" "Because the government would have something to say about that." "On our property?" "Yes, all the rivers and the creeks belong to the government or are under their jurisdictions. Maybe there is a natural little beach and that they can't do anything about it." "Let's hope so. The best news about this one is I think at a very good price." "The killing question! How much is it?" "Twenty thousands! When you compare this one to the five acres at fifty thousands each, I think it's cheap. This one has one hundred and sixty acres." "That is because the five acres are zoned commercial probably. And what about the forth one?" "It's a newer farm with a house almost new, a big barn, seventy cows and a big bull. They're asking three hundreds and fifty thousands dollars for it. There is also a huge German shepherd that comes with it." "Are you interested in that one?" "Not really! " "Do you have a phone number for the little farm?" "Yes, the old man lives in Quebec City." "Do you know if there is power around this property." "Yes, it is written that the power is accessible and the road is cleaned year round. Well, I don't know what you girls are thinking, but I sure would like to walk this one soon." "You know James that we are trusting you for this kind of things." "Give me this phone number Janene and I will call tomorrow morning and that is only because it's too late to call tonight." "All of that wood doesn't scare you?" "On the contrary, I love it." "Can you tell us why?" "What if I keep it my secret for a while?" "We don't have any secret for you." "Ho no, what about my birthday party? Wasn't that kept secret?" "Yes, but this is not the same." "On the contrary, it's exactly the same and it's getting late, we should go to bed now." "I'm surprised you took that long, I began thinking that you forgot. Such a great invitation, no way Jose! Give me a few minutes first I will put Danielle to bed."

"I got to tell you Danielle, I'm very proud of you." "Can you stay for a few minutes more? I'm so excited I would like to be released a little bit." "I can't be long." "Don't waste any time talking go right ahead." "Try not to scream, I don't want Janene to think that she still lost her turn." "Go ahead, pleaseeeeeeeees." "Juicy like you, it's impossible. Good night!" "Good night! Now I'm going to sleep nicely."

I went to the bathroom to clean up a bit and then I went to join Janene who also made nice plans to make me happy. To say happy is to say too little, because I have to admit it, I'm experiencing something that is beyond happiness. I think it's beyond every man's dream.

In the morning right after breakfast I dialled the phone number that Janene gave me.

Allô!" "Allô" "Talk louder my earring is not too good." "I called to find out about the little farm you have near Trois Rivières." "It's for sale." "I know and I'm interested. That is why I called you." "You have to be very interested, because I'm too old to travel that far just for a ride."

"I would like to walk it to see what you've got." "You will have to walk alone, because I can't drag myself anymore." "That's alright. You only have to show me the directions. When can you come this way?" "I can be there on Sunday if it's nice out there. I can be there around noon." "Bring all the necessary papers, because I'm very serious." "What is your name?" "My name is James Prince." "Mine is André Fillion. We need a place to meet." "Do you know where is the Grandma Restaurant?" "I was there quite often and on top of everything, it's on our way. I'll be there at noon on Sunday if I'm still alive." "Come on now, don't play games on me, I want you to see what I'm going to do with this property." "You sound like a gentleman and I can't wait to meet you." "See you on Sunday and be careful."

I went on my construction sites that I've kind of neglected these last few days, duty demands. Everything seemed to be alright so after discussing a few details with the foremen I went home to finish the plans for the mention. I told him that we most likely going to have a triplex to build and that we have to finish all the going work first. He seemed to be happy to have work guaranteed for most of the year. I also knew that he would tell all the others.

At noon all the plans and blue prints were finally done and ready for the demand of the permits, just a question of being legal. I still needed to get the property registered in our names to complete everything. I was sure hoping this wouldn't delay the beginning of the work. I already knew that except for a major problem, it was the piece of land that I was hoping for. After a good dinner I went to present the plans at the building office telling the people that the plan of the land will be there shortly. I just knew I was saving some important time by doing things this way. I also made an appointment with the surveyor who assured me that he will be there when I need him. I was completely ready for this wonderful project. It is not the biggest of my carrier, but surely the one I'm the most proud of to this day. The main reason is very simple, this house won the first price for the house of the year in Canada. The price included a trophy and a wonderful cheque of one hundred thousand dollars. It helps a bit to get rid of a mortgage. At first, I wasn't too sure if I should accept it, because I wanted to keep our place as private as possible. After some discussions with my women they came to the conclusion and they insisted that I should benefit from the product of my imagination. Then I took arrangement with the association to limit the propaganda.

From one thing to another things were rolling pretty fast and the girls asked me to go wait for them at the same place we met a year ago, day for day, because they wanted to renew this wonderful night we had then. So I put on the same suit and I went to lean on the same wall I did a year ago when Danielle first talked to me. A few women came to ask me to dance, but there was no way I would miss the moment when one of my ladies was going to show up. One young woman said to me; "What's the problem, I'm not good enough for you?" "That's not it, I'm just waiting for the femme fatale." "Be careful, she might just be fatal to you." "The ones I want I would die for anytime." "Maybe you're too romantic for our times." "Maybe so, but that's the way I like it."

"May I invite you for a dance sir?" "You sure can pretty lady."

"So, this is it, you like blonds?" "Only if they are fatal. This one is so gorges, she's a killer."

"What is the problem here? " "I refused to dance with her and she's not too happy about it. You sure took a long time you two, where is Danielle?" "She is sitting down at the exact same place I was sat last year." "Did she found a tick truck driver too?" "If he wasn't that tick I might have left with him." "What would you have missed?"

"Stop, I don't even want to think about it. I had such a wonderful year of happiness with you and I meant to tell you while dancing." "I have a hard time believing that you could be happier than me Janene." "You'll have to dance with my best friend too, you know?" "I just can't refuse you anything my sweetie, that's how much I love you." "Where did you learn to speak to women like you do? " "I learn day by day as I live with the two of you.

I'll have to invent a three ways dance partner, because, when I'm with one of you I miss the other and I hate to leave her waiting." "You really love us both, don't you?" "I love enormously both of you, yes. Let's go meet Danielle now."

It was there just as many people than last year if not more and again we had to push our way all the way to the table. Danielle was sitting down with her brother and his girlfriend Sylvia. She had save us two chairs what shouldn't have been too easy with that kind of crowd. Normand, Danielle's brother called me the seducer, which is really not the case.

"You seem to have fun, you two?" "Yes we're having a good time, but here are a bit too many people to my liking."

"I found out that you build nice houses James and I want to have one built eventually." "I don't want you to think that I'm rude or independent or anything like that Normand, but you'll have to contact me at my office for that, because I never mix pleasure with business."

"You were right Danielle." "I told you brother, I know my man."

"This is a nice cha-cha Danielle, do you want to dance?" "Nothing would please me more right now." "Are you sure about that?" "Between you and me, just say almost nothing."

Then the band slowed down a little bit to play the very first piece of music that we danced on last year.

"Did you ask for it?" "No, I thought maybe it was you." "Maybe it's just a fluke or Janene did." "It doesn't matter, it's just as good as the first time. May we live these moments over and over again like then, for it was the beginning of a wonderful adventure. We have a whole life ahead of us and I will do my very best to make it as interesting as possible." "I have to admit I am a little concern about the marriage." "What are you concerned about sweetie?" "I'm not worried about my marriage with you, but I'm afraid that you might have a hard time to marry Janene once you're married to me." "It's very possible that your worry is founded, but what ever happens, I consider myself already married to both of you before God and nobody can change that. Papers are only formalities." "I love you so much it's almost unexplainable." "I know exactly what you're talking about." "Then we understand each other." "I can't wait to take you to bed, do you know it?" "I felt it." "Did you like it?" "As usual, I'm always extremely fine in your arms." "Are we going home early?" "Go dance with Janene another time, she too love to dance with you." "I love dancing with both of you."

The crowd was still very heavy and I was telling myself that if there was ever a fire, we would be cook like rats. I would be absolutely powerless in such a mob. All it would take is that an idiot starts yelling; fire, fire even if there is nothing at all for the crowd to panic. It's my love for the two of them that inspired me to stay away from these high risk places. There is nothing as scaring as the thought of losing your loved ones.

"What is the problem James, you look so worried? Are you alright?" "I'll explain it to you later if you don't mind."

When we got to our table Janene was gone. Danielle asked her brother if he knew where she was, being herself wondering about it when Janene suddenly showed up. Janene looked quite upset and she was followed by a man who was apologizing all the way to our table. As soon as she was close to us she turned around to face him and yelled loudly; "Get to F out of my face before I use my claws on yours." "I didn't wa……. " "Go away I told you."

I got up to face the man and I told him looking him straight in his eyes and I said; "You've heard the lady so go away while you can." "Alright, alright, I'm leaving. No point yelling so much."

"Calm down now Janene, it's over. What the heck happened to make you so mad?" "He didn't want to let me go when I wanted to.

He forced me to insist and I don't like to be force in what so ever." "I kind of understand that a man would want to hold you back on the dance floor. The least we can say is that he's got good taste." "Good taste my ass, I can't be forced, that's all." "Would you like to go somewhere else?" "No, I just want to dance with you again, would you?" "Of course I would, but only if you calm down. I'm little scare of your claws." "Very funny, let's go."

We danced a mambo, a tango, a nice samba, a Rumba, and we were just starting a nice slow when I felt a touch on my left shoulder. I kept dancing anyway, but that touch became more and more insisting.

"James, it's him again." "Keep dancing and pull yourself back a little, would you?" "What are you going to do?" "Just trust me, you'll see. Keep your eyes wide opened and at the same time he'll put his hand on me again pull yourself back very quickly, ok?" "Ok!"

I was waiting very patiently the moment he was going to touch me one more time and when he did it, Janene who did exactly as I asked her to do, pulled herself back quickly and at the same time I grabbed the fingers of this man who found himself on his knees making all kinds of faces. A few people started to scream and within a few seconds a couple of doormen were on the spot too. One of them asked Janene what happened and with no hesitation she told him that this man was harassing her. The two men grabbed him and showed him the door, which will be banished for him for a couple of years to come.

"You will never cease to impress me, will you?" "This is not something I like to talk about Janene, because this is my strength, the surprise and the fact that my enemy doesn't know what I'm capable of. You see this guy didn't have a clue of all this and he was taken by surprise. He is almost twice my size and he thought he had nothing to fear. Now I just hope nobody will talk about this at all. What if we get out of here now?" "He might be waiting for us outside." "Don't worry, he had his lesson. The world is full of this kind of hazards, we just have to be ready for them."

I walked Janene to our table and then I took off for a few minutes because, I wanted to know this man's name. I went to talk to the doormen who took care of this individual and they said they couldn't tell me his name.

"If this man is a treat to my family, I have the right to know what his name is. If I have to call the police to find out who he is, I will."

One of them knew me enough to know that I won't hesitate a single minute to do it.

"We don't want to get the police involved in this, just for such insignificant matter. It's never too good for our reputation to get the police involved. His name is Bernard Sinclair." "Thank you!" "You never learned it from us." "That's fine, I got what I want."

I quickly went back to our table to find all of them in a passionate conversation.

"Where did you go? You seem concerned" "I just needed a little information, that's all. I think we should go now. Are you guys hungry? Maybe we could go to a restaurant." "Thanks the same, but we have prepared a little snack at home before we left if you're interested naturally." "That's fine with me, let's go. Ho, one more thing before we go, make sure that no one else but me is following you."

We drove home without any problem. They had prepared everything before they left and that was the reason for them to be a little late at the dance. They had organized a birthday like no one else has ever done, I'm sure. On the table there was everything you can imagine to please the mouth. Suddenly Danielle got up and went to run the water in the tub.

"Do you remember last year?" "I will never forget it for as long as I live." "We would like to repeat it just in case it happens some day. We just want to refresh your memory." "Which one will get the shower this time?" "It's Danielle's turn." "Don't tell me that you still need a simple of my love for the laboratory. You're the only ones with whom I sleep since I met you."

"No, we trust you one hundred per cent, but Danielle doesn't know what it's like to be showered that way. That will be fine if she likes surprises, because it goes out without warnings. Go slow Janene, I got lots of time and tonight I do more than just look."

For the rest you people already know what happened, because it's the same thing than last year. When the morning came at around ten, I turned on the TV to take the last news as I almost always do.

"Oh my God ! Oh my God !"

I returned very quickly to the bedroom to talk with Janene.

"Let me sleep a bit longer, would you James?" "Janene, there are bad news." "What is it?" "The guy we had trouble with last night, he was arrested." "You call that bad news? It's good for him, he deserved it." "He returned to the club with a gun, I think he was seeking revenge. I also think he was looking for me." "What?" "He was looking for us." "He's crazy, they're going to lock him up. I'm not so sure about that." "What are we going to do?" "For as long that he is in jail there is no danger, but when he's out, that's another story. I don't think he knows where we live, but then again, we don't know for sure. I have to go to the police station to find out more about this. By acting like he did he made death threats. Do you realize that? He will get a few years. I'm sure too that there were a lot of witnesses. His name is Bernard Sinclair." "I think I know this name." "Try to remember, every detail could be important."

I got dressed and I went to the station to find more on that case if it was possible.

"Can I speak to the officer that is on Sinclair's case, please?" "Do you have a special reason for this?" "I have a reason to believe that he was after me last night." "What is your name?" "My name is James Prince." "That is not what he told us. He told us that he was looking for one of the doorman who bullied him." "Alright, maybe I made a mistake. Excuse-me!" "There is no problem."

I returned to the condo, but I was certainly not convinced of what I just heard. There was something very suspicious about the whole thing and I knew that I had to keep my eyes opened and my ears alert.

"Girls, it's me, are you up?" "James, is that you? We might be in danger." "What makes you think that?" "Did you say that his name is Bernard Sinclair?" "Yes, why?" "He might just be Raymond's brother, doctor Raymond Sinclair's brother." "So that means that it wasn't just a hazard last night, maybe it was a plot for revenge. I think that you girls should think of moving out of here. They both know where you live and it's not secure for you here anymore. It's best that you put this apartment for sell as soon as possible." "Where could we go?" "My place is very modest, but I have room for both of you and it will be safer." "If it's good enough for you, it's good enough for us. It is only for a few months, our new house should be ready for September. If you pack everything I could use my men to load the truck. You could be out of here in a single day even if it's hurting. You'll have to be careful at all time, you know that, don't you?" "Yes, we know. You said that the new house could be ready within six months?" "Yes, I already asked for the permit." "But you need to have the plan and blue prints. I presented them with the demand of the permit already. I spent the whole week on that project." "What a sweetheart you are." "Do you want to see them?" "You got them?" "Of course I do, I made them. Just wait a few minutes, I'll get them." "Be careful you too." "Don't worry, I will be. It's me girls, you can open. Take a look at this." "What a beautiful thing. You made this?" "I did." "But you're quite an artist. I only designed what you asked me. All you have left to do is to choose the colors and the furniture to decorate it. Here is the flooring plan." "It's even better than what I had anticipated. A very large kitchen with an Island and a large number of cupboards. A large living room just like I like it. Three big bedrooms! What is this?" "There is a bathroom between each bedroom." "What a marvellous idea!" "There is an insulated panel in each wall. This is the same material that they build freezers with. If you want to know how efficient it is, you just have to put a battery operated radio on high volume in a freezer and shut the cover. Danielle especially really needs walls like those." "Look at the size of these windows. The balcony makes the whole link of the house. How long is it?" "Fifty-eight feet long!" "It's almost a race track. Kids will just love to ride it with their bikes." "After what happened last night at the club, I think I would like to have a dance floor in one of the basements, with your permission, of course. Take your time and discuss it between the two of you. You've got six months to make up your mind. It would also make a nice place for kids to play in on the rainy days. The heat system is made of many pipes running in the floors where hot water is circulating all the time. Each place will also have a slow wood burner just in case the power goes off for some reasons. That system will function the same way a conventional hot air system operates. Only it will operate on batteries. The batteries system will be able to operate and supply us with all the power we need for a whole week before the need of a generator. The walls between my place and yours and the floor between the garage and my place will be done with reinforced concrete capable to resist a medium explosion. We never know what can happen with cars. There is a fan system also capable to send all the smoke outside in case of a fire. The walls and the communicating doors are also fire proof. There is an intercom system in the whole house that works together with the sound system. You might lose the sight of me, but not the sound of me. Inside each window there is a blind that comes down as soon as you turn the light on." "You're not serious?" "Ho yes, I am. Of course there is a vacuum system in the whole house. I will have a cold room at the end of the garage and also a place to put fire wood. Each one of us can enter our own place from the garage. That's about it. Ho yes, each bathroom is big enough to include your laundry machines or if you like it better I could install them in your basement. If you choose the latter one, I will make a shoot for your dirty laundry that we're going to keep within our family I'm sure. I will find a bathtub like you have here if it is what you want. Why are you so quiet?" "It's simple, we are stunned. Everything is there, there's nothing to add and nothing more to say. How do you do it?" "It is totally genial." "Come on Janene it's just a house. You like?" "If we like it?" "Do we have enough money for all of this?" "I think so." "What is the big number?" "I got it here somewhere." "It is a bit more than I initially thought. It comes to five hundred and forty seven thousand and two hundred. You don't pay anything for the garage, because it's under my quarters. Each share of you comes to two hundred and eight thousand, eight hundred." "We are ten thousand dollars short and we don't have the land yet." "You both have an excellent job and the banks will go out of their way to lend you the money. We'll talk about that later if you don't mind. For the land, you don't worry, I'll buy it, in fact, I will meet tomorrow with the old men. I got to meet him by noon and I will have diner with him at the restaurant. I will walk the land and I will take a decision afterward. If I like it I will buy it, but I will put your names on the contract as owners as well. It will be ours at even shares. All I ask is the right to use it my own way." "I see no problem with that." "Me neither." "So we all agree." "Tell me James, why are you doing all this?" "Everything I buy since we are together would be consider equal share from the court point of view anyway if we ever separate. Might as well do it now." "God as reunited us and no one will separate. It's there for better or worst." "You will have to come and sign for the permits too, because we will be owners and responsible for each of our quarters and it's better that way." "But we still don't have enough money for all this." "Is that what you want?" "It is a lot more that we were hoping for." "Are you absolutely sure?" "Yes, we are." "I don't think so. Sure, also mean sour in French. But I know that you are both very sweet." "Ha, ha, ha, very funny." "Here is what I suggest you do. You have between the two of you four hundred and ten thousand and you need four hundred and eighteen thousand, is that right?" "That's right." "Then you need to go see your bank manager and borrow each of you a big one hundred thousand dollars." "What?" "You heard me. Never let yourself go dry if you can do otherwise. Desmarais made himself a multi millionaire with bank's money and you can do the same. Banks lend up to ninety and ninety-five % on properties and in your case you would only borrow a lean twenty-five per cent from which you would only use ten per cent for your actual needs. You keep approximately ten thousand in you bank account for your own needs and place the rest at fifteen per cent for a loan that cost you five per cent which is the rate of preferential customers. This way rather then pay for a loan, you get pay for it." "But this kind of deals scare me." "Even if I take responsibility for anything that could happen?" "Well then, I close my eyes." "Make an appointment quickly with your bank manager and I will take care of the rest. So, you had fun? Me too, because I don't work on Saturday. What do we have for supper?" "Are you hungry?" "A little! Everything will be ready in five minutes; I too don't like to work on Saturday. I got everything ready yesterday." "Do you have a good movie for the evening? I would love necking with both of you tonight." "That can be arranged my man, but maybe you'll find us a bit sticky." "That's good. Sticky yesterday and today and forever, stick with me girls, I love it."

I'm not too sure if it was because my women were toady and charming, but I didn't find the movie interesting at all. They kind of brought up the temperature and something else too.

"I'm not too sure where I'm at right now, who's turn is it?" "It's Danielle's, go ahead, don't waste any time, I want some too." "Well ok, then Janene would you run the water in the tub, we will need it and this way it will go faster. Come Danielle, don't let Janene wait too long, she seems to be very hungry"

That was very quick indeed, because we were both ready to explode right from the beginning. Then we jumped in the tub where we soap each other lovingly.

"It's your turn tonight to get me for the night, are you going to wait?" "If you're not too long, I'm going to watch the movie we were supposed to watch all together." "Then I'll come to watch the end of it with you. See you in a bit, I love you."

I went to spend thirty-five minutes with Janene and when I left her she was contempt and ready to sleep for the night. I watched the rest of the movie with Danielle, which was not so dull after all. Afterward we went to bed and continued what we had started earlier. I was very satisfied with myself on that particular Saturday, mainly because I succeeded to make them forget about the tremendous threat that was hovering over our heads with the Sinclairs.

The next day at noon on that Sunday I met with M Fillion just as planned, a man that you wish you always known and have as a friend. After a very good meal at the restaurant we got into my vehicle and he guided me to the property that I was interested in.

"I wish I was still young just to walk with you in that wood one more time. I hope you brought a gun with you. You might encounter some wolves, we saw some before, you know?" "Yes, I thought of it." "This nice piece of land wouldn't be for sell if only I could walk like I used to.

You must know that." "Do you know your neighbours on both sides?" "Yes, they are good people and they too are getting old." "Do you think they would sell their properties too?" "I'm sure they would sell if they could. They tried to sell before, but no one wants those abandoned farms so far away from everything. Besides, they're not profitable. You can only starve on a farm like that." "You're not a very good salesman, are you?" "I'm honest and I tell things the way they are." "You said that there is a little river on that land, didn't you? Is there any fish in it?" "My friend, I ate a lot of good trout." "Is there enough water to make a little beach?" "It's already there just natural and there is about six feet deep of water. It's also there that I took all the nice twelve inches trout." "Any deer?" "I promise that you'll never have to go anywhere else to hunt." "Interesting ! You said that you want twenty thousand for this land, didn't you?" "This is the asking price, yes." "How is the entrance situated, North, South, East or West?" "The entrance is South! How important that is?"

"To me it is." "Did you bring the land title?" "Yes !" "Is there any chance or I should say risk I get lost in that wood?" "Not really, there is a road on each side and a very good fence at the end of the property. You can't get lost, you go all the way up North and come back all the way South, simple as that." "It should take me a few hours." "If it wasn't for the undergrowth on the road, we could go all the way with your vehicle." "I'll have a lot of cleaning up to do if I buy. You can wait for me in the vehicle, I'll leave you the keys so you can listen to the radio and if you get cold, you can start it."

When I enter the wood it was nice and sunny, but without any warning all of a sudden, it started snowing to the point I couldn't see the skies and neither the ground. I was gone for more than two and a half hours when my old friend began to worry seriously. I start to pray that he doesn't leave the van on the spur of the moment out of compassion to come to my rescue. It's always easier to look for one person than to look for two and besides, for him to walk in that weather condition would have probably killed him. But he did what he should do and that was to blow the horn until he sees me. The least I can say is that he was quite relieved to see me again. I was out of the bush, but not out of the storm yet. In no time at all there was more than eight inches of snow on the ground. My father often mentioned the March snow storms, luckily I had good tires and I had a front wheel drive vehicle. I was also convinced that I would have to buy a tractor as soon as possible. The problem was to turn around without getting stock in that deep snow. My fear was founded, because after I backed up while turning, I got stock really good where I couldn't move either way.

"Hope you have a shovel. I'm not very strong anymore, but maybe I can push a little." "It won't be necessary, I got what I need." "Do you really think so?" "No, I'm sure." "We'll see."

I then got out and took the shovel to clear the snow that was up to the bottom of the doors and was blocking the wheels. I put the shovel away and I got back in, but that wet snow made it so slippery that there was no traction at all.

"You'll need me to either push or to get behind the wheel." "Even if you get behind the wheel, you would have to stop to pick me up and we would be at the starting point again. I got better than that."

I got out again and I put what I should under the front wheels and came back in again.

"Hold on, we're on are way." "Oh, you believe that?" "Yes I do." "I'll be damned. What did you do?" "I just put a shingle under each wheel. Once you're gone, you just can't stop, you have to keep going. You just have to put the rough side down of those shingles so they don't slip and the trick is done. It's cheap and very efficient and it's not worth stopping to pick them up." "Don't say anymore, I'm convinced. We sure learn at all ages, don't we?" "How good are they to open the roads in this part of the country?" "We never had any problem. You might just have to call the council if you're not happy with what is done." "You can not drive back home in that kind of weather and you can stay at my place tonight, this way we could see the lawyer tomorrow." "does that mean you're buying, but you couldn't see it all?" "I saw what I needed to see and I am happy to take it away from you." "Don't tell me that you found gold." "Gold wouldn't make me as happy as this property will." "Well ! It's true that you were serious." "Are you coming to my place?" "I don't want to disturb. It would be better than at the hotel, I think." "It settled then, I'll take you to my place and then I'll go pick up a couple of my friends and I'll be right back."

So I took him to my place and I told him to make himself at home. I then went to get my two favourite girls mainly because I didn't want them to be left alone for the night knowing perfectly well they weren't safe in their apartment.

"Hi, It's me." "It's you James? We were worried about you with that snow storm outside." "And I was worried for you. You are coming to sleep at my place tonight, because I don't think this place is any longer safe for you. Really, you believe that?" "Yes I do.

This Sinclair who was looking for us the other night will still be looking for us." "But you said he was in jail." "He can be out of it as soon as somebody pays his bail and that could be sooner than we wish for. As far as I'm concerned he might be out already and I'm not ready to take any risk with your well-being. Did you pack your things?" "No, we didn't think it was that urgent." "Listen girls, this guy came after us the other night with a loaded gun and you don't think it is urgent." "How did it go on the property? I don't think it was too easy with that snow storm." "I had enough time to see what I wanted to see and I'm buying it. The seller is at my place waiting for us." "You left the blue prints over here, do you want them now?" "Yes, I need them. What time are you working tomorrow?" "Janene is working daytime and I work in the evening." "We don't have solid proof, but I'm pretty sure they are going to harm one of us and yet maybe every one so take what you need for the night and we will come to take the rest tomorrow. Don't worry, I'll take care of everything. Danielle, you should advertise the condo as soon as tomorrow and it should go very quick, because, there are not enough on the market. You should contact your bank manager as soon as you can also." "I will." "Are you ready?" "We are." "Let's go. Let me go down first and see that everything is alright. I'll let you know through the intercom." "Forgive us, we didn't think that it was so serious." "It's my fault, I didn't want neither of you to be too worried, but the danger is real. When an individual is crazy enough to enter a bar and threats to shoot someone, it's serious and we cannot take it too lightly." "Now I'm scared." "It's better that you are scared a bit and careful than not scared and too boldly, but everything will be fine, I'm sure. You'll have to be careful at work too, we don't really know what doctor Sinclair is capable of." "It won't be easy, he's always working directly with us." "Keep your eyes opened, that's all. Alright, I'm going down. See you in a bit."

Everything went fine that night and so were the next few weeks. We got home to find my old friend sleeping on the couch in front of the TV set. It must have been a very long day for him with all the stress of the day on top of his trip from Quebec City. We let him sleep until the supper was ready. I offered meat sauce spaghetti to my young ladies and they accepted that with a smile knowing very well I was the host for the evening. It was an ancient meal served in the modern time. You should have seen the eyes of the old man when he saw my two beautiful guests.

"I'm I still alive or dead and in heaven? I got the impression that I am in front of two angels."

He gave us a good laugh. He was old, but not blind and he knew how to appreciate the beauties of this world. He also seemed to wonder what I was doing with two of such beautiful women. I didn't feel the need to inform him about it. Once we discussed the price of the land and came to an accord, I showed him the plan of the house that we intend to build on that property and he could not believe his own eyes. Since he was such a poor salesman I decided to sell myself this piece of land to myself. He came down to ten thousand dollars, but I made him a cheque for twenty thousand. One more time he seemed all confused and still wondered if he was still a member of this world. I also paid for the registration and all other expenses and I wanted him to be able to cash his cheque the same day, but the notary public said no.

"The money will be deposit in a truss account and will go in M Fillion account as soon as we know that the tittles are clear of liens and the land really belongs to him and only him. Andre quickly understood that it was the normal procedure. Everything went on the same day anyway. It was obvious that he really loved this property and the only reason for selling was because he could not take care of it anymore. He was one of the rare chosen people to be invited at the inauguration of our house.

"I'm almost eighty and I never met someone like you. There is something with you that is not like everybody else." "Maybe it's because I walk with God and God is with me." "Ho, Him, I don't really believe in." "Maybe you don't really know Him." "We were told that He sees everything, but you didn't see your way out of the snow storm." "Did I get lost?"

"No, but it's most likely because I blew the horn." "I would say that He gave you the occasion, the opportunity to make yourself useful for someone in distress even at your age, you who is getting weaker and sometimes thinks that is good for nothing." "It could be one way to see things." "Where do you think that our thoughts and our ideas come from?" "I don't really know, but they most likely are within us." "On the contrary, I know for sure that the spirits are speaking to us, and some of us know how to listen and others don't. Some of us listen to the good spirits and others listen to the bad ones." "Where did you get such information? In Mathew 16, 17, Jesus said to Peter; "Blessed are you Peter, son of Jona, because it is not the flesh and blood that revealed this to you, but my Father which is in heaven." And then practically in the same conversation Jesus said to Peter again; "Get behind me, Satan: you are offensive to me for your thoughts are not from God, but from men."

"Never in my whole life I heard someone talk like you do." "That is just because you didn't listen to Jesus. Many people think they are atheist because they don't believe in men who are supposed to tell the truth, they do it without making sure those same men are really from God. The ones who lied especially about the word of God are not from God, but from the devil and they are like the sand by the sea." "Nice meeting you James, it's a pleasure to do business with you."

That's what he told me shaking my hand warmly. He took off afterward sadly I could tell. I wished I could spend more time with him, but I had many more things to do. I couldn't wait to join Danielle who had a lot of things to do on her own. I also went to the police station to find out the last move in the Sinclair's affair. There is when I found out that the criminal was out on bail paid by his brother, the famous doctor. I was pretty sure he was going to try something else again, but I had no Idea what to expect. I met with Danielle at my place at lunch time.

"How did it go at the bank?" "Pretty good I think, he said it will be no problem. Are you too busy to kiss me today?" "I'm so sorry, but I have so many things on my mind at the present time. I still have to go rent a truck.

"I gave it a lot of thoughts and I don't think it will be necessary." "What do you mean? You don't want to move in anymore?" "That's not it, but I don't think we need all of those things. You have basically everything we need right here. We could just take the food and a few other things that we need, but for the rest it could just stay in place. You know as well as I do that a furnished apartment sells easier than an empty one." "You might be right. Let's forget about the truck and we can move the little you need in my van. Did you put the ad in the paper?" "Yes I did, in the paper and on the internet." "That's a very good idea. Did you talk to Janene?" "Yes, she's fine. How things with you?" "Fine, the property is ours." "Is that right? I'm so happy." "M Fillion is on his way back home." "He might just be a bad salesman, but you are a bad buyer, you lost ten thousand dollars by your own fault." "How much did you ask for your condo?" "Two hundred and twenty thousands." "What would you say if someone would pay it without asking any question?" "It would be wonderful." "This is it, do to others what you would want others do for you." "Another good lesson!"

"It's free." "What do we do next?" "You have two hours in front of you, might as well go get your things at the apartment." "Ok, let's go." "I got to call the foreman to cancel the moving assignment." "The real superman is not in fiction, it's you." "Ho, come on, don't embarrass me, ok? I don't do anything that is not normal." "But you do so much, no one ever saw something like that." "You're exaggerating, let's go."

As soon as we were back with all their things that they needed Danielle went to work. She certainly wasn't in an enviable position. Anybody can say what he wants, it's not that easy to pay good for the bad that we get. She had to be strong to go through this. We couldn't even talk to anybody about the whole situation for fear to be sued for defamation. The situation wasn't easy at all. Then I went to my construction sites to find out that the work was in good progress.

Raoul, the Foreman met with the new owners who all seem to be happy with our masterpieces.

I didn't stay there too long, because I wanted to be home to welcome Janene to her new living quarters. After I informed her of all the activities of the day I went to make supper.

Chapter 4

"What are you making?" "I'm making a fricassee. Did you ever heard of it?" " Yes, but I don't remember having it." "I like Africa, see. You must since you're making one. Did you ever go to Africa? Africa, see !" "Ha you ! Comic, very funny! When everything is almost cooked I'll add the dumplings and we'll have to wait another twenty minutes for it to be ready to eat. I just love those dumplings, especially when they are well done so if you don't really like them you can leave them to me. Bingo, the lady is served." "Wow, this is good. You'll have to show me how to do this so I can make it for you some day. I think that Danielle and I are lucky, you're a good man to marry. I don't think that will be easy even If I love you with all my body, my heart and my soul. No matter what, I'll do everything that is possible for that to happen, but I tell you right now, there is no way for me to join a religion, because it would mean making a deal with the devil to me. Salomon was the wisest king on earth and he had a fabulous wealth, but he lost everything because, he prostituted himself to the foreign gods and religions of his last wives. With the help of my true God I won't make the same mistake." "Are you telling me that you're not going to marry me?" "Not at all, I'm telling you that I'm not going to join any religion even though I love you with all my heart." "The most important is that you love me. All I know is that I couldn't live without you." "I couldn't live without you either." "No matter what, if you get rid of our problems the way you got rid of that big ass hole the other night, everything will be fine." "I wish I could be as sure as you." "Why, is there a problem?" "He's already out of jail, because your doctor bailed him out." "The son of a b..... What are we going to do?" "We'll have to wait that he compromise himself, unfortunately until then we won't be able to react." "In the mean time we have to live in fear and uncertainty every day." "Exactly, we don't know what they'll do next." "You said they?" "Yes, I think that the doctor might be as dangerous as his brother, maybe even more." "Does Danielle know it?" "I told her to keep her eyes opened at all time." "Changing the subject how did it go with the property?" "It's ours. I bought it today and everything is finalized." "Is that true? Ho, I'm so happy. That means you will start building our house very soon." "I will as soon as the ground is defrosted. I will buy a backhoe to remove the snow and I will install an eating tarp, one of my inventions to defrost the ground. I can't wait to see how it works." "A backhoe, that's a lot of money, isn't it?" "It's nearly one hundred thousand for a new one, but I have a lot of work for it with the excavation plus all the undergrowth. There is a mile of road on both side to clear and we cannot stay in the country without at least a tractor. A backhoe is a lot better and it's a machine that will pay by itself. I paid my excavator almost twenty-five thousand a year in the last three years. This kind of machine is good for at least thirty years. Believe me, it's a good deal." "Are you sure that you're not going to be short for the house though? According to your numbers you basically build our house for the cost and without any profit." "Where did you get this information?" "You left the blue prints at our place yesterday and we asked another contractor how much it would be, because we thought you didn't estimate this house high enough. The other contractor said that it wasn't the final price, but it would be at least seven hundred thousands. There is a difference of more than one hundred and fifty thousands." "Well I didn't want to make any profit with my spouses and I'm sure that if I need any help you both going to be there for me. I also made all the calculations and I'm sure if I'm short of a bit of money there will be friends to help me out. My quarters are not very big which don't cost a heck of a lot and this house here will pay just about everything including the backhoe." "I think that you are a business' genius." "I'm not sure of that especially according to Danielle and M Fillion." "What make you say that?" "I paid twenty thousands for the property, but I could have got it for ten." "What is the matter with you?" "He was vulnerable and I didn't want to take advantage of him." "It's all to you credit and I'm sure that God will return it to you." "Now I know that you know Him well.

I don't know how it is for you, but I'm extremely tired." "Come and lay down, I'll give you a massage." "Your hands are incredibly soft. It's very nice." "James ! James ! Are you sleeping? No treat for me tonight. There is no treat, there is no treat, there is no treat for me tonight. I hope I wouldn't have to sing that to often. Well, I guess I'll put a movie on then."

Janene felt asleep too on another couch in front of the TV. She had covered me up with a bedspread. It was the first time in a whole year that I couldn't satisfy one of them but, believe me, it was not without any regrets.

Since there is a reason for everything, the only fact that she was near the door allowed Janene to wake up quickly when Danielle arrived, she had forgotten to take a key for the house. I had shivers just thinking that she just might have decided to go sleep in the condo all by herself if she couldn't get in. I took advantage of the situation to warn her again to not ever take any risk. I would rather lose a window.

"What is James doing on the couch?" "He was extremely tired and he fell asleep right there. I thought it was best to let him rest." "You're not going to kill him with love making Janene, are you?. I know he's strong, but control yourself, would you?" "No Danielle, I didn't get any treat tonight, but it's not because I didn't want it." "He should go sleep in his bed, he would be more comfortable." "He sleeps so well that I think it's best to let him stay there."

They both went to bed without any treat that night but, I went to join Danielle at four thirty in the morning, although I was very careful not to wake her up. When we did wake up, Janene was already gone to work. After breakfast Danielle went on the computer to read her Emails. There were as usual a big number of messages most of them none senses when suddenly her eyes stop on one a little more interesting. She yelled for me to come to take a look on the screen which scared me at first.

"What's going on Danielle, you've scared me." "Nevermind, just read this."

"Very interested in your condominium, please don't sell before I had a chance to see it. If it is still available, I'll take a plane tonight and I will meet you tomorrow at noon. I'm waiting for an answer, Laurent !"

"What do you think of that James?" "He might be a potential buyer, what are you waiting for to give him an answer? Make sure you don't let him think that you absolutely have to sell." "I'll let you read my answer before I send it, what you think?" "As you wish sweetie."

"The condo is still available, but the demand is very high in this town. If you are very serious and I can put my trust in you, I'll wait until tomorrow noon before I make any decision, Danielle."

"What do you think of this James?" "It's perfect, it's short and it let him believe that if he really wants it, he is better to move fast. That's what you need to send him to make him move on it. Send it, we'll see what happens." "It's gone. Do you have anymore tea?" "Yes, I'll bring it to you right away. Do you want any biscuits with it?" "That would be nice, thank you." "Here, madam is served." "You are a treasure." "Ho come on, that's nothing." "You have no idea what it means for us women, do you? " "Ho yes I do." "All right, tell me what it is then." "It's a jar of good treats which I can stick my face into." "That's pretty well it. Hey, come to see this, I got an answer."

"Give me the name and address of your bank and I'll send you five thousands dollars to the desk in your name. If I'm there on time that money will go as a deposit towards the condo, if not it will be just a gift to you, Laurent." "Internet is unbelievably quick. Give him the OK and we'll go to the bank to see if the money is there."

Danielle gave the answer with all the information that he needed for the transaction and then we went to the bank.

"You don't really have to come with me James." "Ho, you think so? What if it was a set up? What if it was one of the Sinclairs who wrote to you?" "Gees, I never thought of that.

We don't really know who's this offer is coming from, do we?" "From now on I'll be your bodyguard. I'll take you to work and I'll pick you up after, if I say get down, you hit the floor, if I say run, you run, understood?" "Yes, it's very clear." "We can't even go to the police without being laugh at. We can only count on us and on us alone." "I understood, I understood, let's go." "Prevention is better than cure even for a special nurse like you."

So we went to the bank as planned to find the money as agreed. That scared me even more, because I said to myself, if this guy is ready to lose five thousand dollars to ambush Danielle that means he'll go to any link to hurt her.

The next day a man in his fifties showed up at the indicated address where he came down a white limo. He was a giant build like a football player. He must be six foot six or more and weigh at least two hundred and fifty pounds. He asked right away to see the condo telling us that he was in extreme hurry.

"Hi, I'm Laurent." "I'm Danielle and this is my husband James." "Please let's go see this thing right away, would you?" "Yes, it's on the sixth floor."

All four of us went to the elevator. His chauffeur who is just as huge was following him just as if he was his bodyguard. I wondered if they were from the mafia or else from the government, which is about the same. One way or the other the situation was scary. As soon as they got in, they went all around the apartment searching the closets testing the beds on and under and all of this without saying a word. I was thinking that I might have to use my marshal art when suddenly Laurent opened his mouth to say;

"What would say if I give you three hundreds thousands for the condo and all the furniture? You would just take your personal belongings." "I would have to talk to my partner."

"No, we agree sir." "But James!" "We have a deal sir." "Laurent Charron is my name. Alright then, my agent will contact you within two hours. I want to move in no later than tomorrow. You will give him the, all the keys please." "He will get them sir and all the personal things will also be out of here by midnight. Is that good enough?" "That will be fine. Good then, we have to go, good day." "Good day sir!"

They went on their way and I had in front of me a lady who was really concerned, completely disconcerted and with big questioning eyes.

"But James, Janene will want to kill me." "Why? To make her more money in one hour than she makes in a whole year? I don't think so." "But we should talk to her first." "This man had no time to waste, it was then or never. How much did the furniture cost you?" "About fifteen thousands if I remember well." "That's what I thought, but he's giving you ninety thousands for it. I don't know his reasons and I don't think I want to know, but this man is in extreme hurry to find a place and he wants it all furnished and both of you are richer by seventy-five thousands." "You are the one who deserves it, I would have lost it." "Surely if you'd insisted to make him wait, and that's why I stepped in. Forgive me?" "Forgive you for what, making us richer? What would we do without you?" "The exact same thing than before." "Before, I don't want to think about it."

We went home to wait for the phone call that was important to us. It was not very long, within fifteen minutes we had an appointment at the lawyer's office.

"Where are the papers for the condo?" "They are at the lawyer's office." "But where is your copy?" "It's there at the lawyer's office. We thought it was the safest place to leave it." "My God but!" "What is the problem?" "You better pray that this man is an honest man." "Why? He is a lawyer." "Danielle, if this man wanted to, this condo is already in his name and there is absolutely nothing you could do about it."

"That is impossible." "Ho yes it is. I have known a notary public in Victoriaville who was dishonest and I had to pay the interests on the land twice.

I took him to court to be told by the judge that he was sorry for my lost, but because I had no proof that I paid the first time, I had to pay again. The judge said that I most likely paid, because the interests are usually paid before the principal and I had my receipt for the principal payment. The lawman said I didn't need a receipt, because he was going to right it in the contract. There you are, he was a lawman. I heard much later that he was bared from office, but that never gave me my money back." "That would be quite a shot to gain seventy-five thousands in one day and lose three hundred thousands." "Don't laugh, it's very possible." "I don't, I'm rather nervous." "Papers like those you put them in a safe either at home or at the bank, but never, never in a place where you could never see them again. Janene and I trust this man." "It's alright to trust people, but it's not alright to put yourself in such a vulnerable position. Take for example, what could happen if this man died and the one who took over his practice was Doctor Sinclair?" "We would lose everything, you're right again." "Of course I'm right. Don't you ever do anything like this again. Let's hope that everything is alright, otherwise our beautiful project is gone with the wind. I hope that we'll be there before anyone else to ask for the papers. Don't cry Danielle, but you have to understand that most of the business people of this world take advantage of the vulnerability of the weak." "I know, I saw what could happened to the poor M Fillion if you wanted to." "Here we are. I beg you darling, what ever happens stay calm, would you?" "I will be, don't worry." "Let's go."

We went in and even though we were twenty minutes ahead of time, they were already waiting for us to come in. That was good news, because it meant that we were still in the picture.

"Everything is fine Danielle." "Are you sure?" "Yes I am."

No point saying that she was quite relieved to hear this. Everything went smoothly and all that was missing was Janene signature. As soon as we were out of this building I called Janene on my cell phone.

"Here's Hôtel Dieu hospital." "Allô, may I speak to Janene please?" "Just a minute!"

"Here is Janene." "Hi Janene!" "Do you have a few minutes?" "It's you James. Is everything alright?" "Yes, everything's fine. If I wanted to buy all your furniture, how much would you sell it to me for ?" "I don't know, I never thought of it. I was with Danielle when we bought it and I think we paid around fifteen thousands." "How much would you sell it to me?" "I don't know, ten, twelve thousands maybe." "What would you say if I can get you ninety thousands for it?" "I'd say that you're mocking me." "Not at all, do you know where is the Tremblai lawyer's office?" "Yes, it's there that we got the contract made for our condo." "It's sold and I'd like you to meet me there after work, would you?" "Of course I will, but are you sure?" "Yes it's sold, all is missing is your signature." "I'll be there." "How is it at work?" "Everything is fine with me, but you know who is working tonight." "Alright, I'll tell Danielle. You'll have to work a few hours tonight too." "That's fine, I feel good. I had a full night sleep." "I'm sorry, I didn't want to let you down." "You needed your sleep, it's understandable and forgivable." "See you in a bit. It might be possible that I meet you when you come out, because I'm taking Danielle there to work. Bye !" "Bye !"

Once I had driven Danielle to work, I went to the Tremblai's office to wait for Janene who was in shortly after me. As soon as all the papers were signed and that we had all the documents in hands I asked Janene to wait for me outside for a few minutes. She seemed a bit confused with my demand, but she nevertheless left me alone with the lawyer.

"Mr Tremblai, you are a serious lawman, aren't you?" "I think I am, yes." "How is it then that you left those two girls without any protection?" "They were under my personal protection from their own demand M Prince." "What could have happened if you'd died and the one who took over wasn't honest?" "All this are only suppositions." "Yes, they are suppositions that could have lead to the lost of three hundred thousands dollars for those two women and this is unacceptable. You have the obligation to protect your clients against everyone including themselves." "Would that be all M Prince?" "That's all, but don't force me to come to testify against you Mr Tremblai, because I will without any hesitation."

Janene who wondered what I was fabricating behind her back kind of force my hand to know what was going on.

"Because of his way to do business you both could have lost everything and that is five years of your income." "But we asked him to keep our papers safely, because we didn't know where to put them." "It was his professional duty to protect you against yourselves. It's easy for anyone to say; put them in a safe at home or at the bank or else make a copy of it and leave one at your parent's home. It makes me mad just to think that you could have lost everything when you deserve the best possible security and protection. Enough of that now! What if we go get the rest of your personal belonging? We only have a few hours ahead of us and we have to give them the keys before eight o'clock tonight." "I can't believe this, ninety thousands for our furniture. All this is real, you sure that I'm not dreaming?" "It's written in black and white on your contract and the money will be in your bank account within a day or two, plus the contract will be put in a safe place, believe me. Danielle wanted to talk to you before giving him an answer, but the buyer had no time to wait, it was kind of then or never situation, there is when I stepped in and decided for you." "You did the right thing, but why didn't Danielle take the decision herself?" "She's got a lot of respect for you. You girls are so close it's something I never ever heard of in my life." "You can say it again, it's just like; Always and Forever."

We picked up a dozen of cardboard boxes and we went to pick up the rest of their things at the apartment. Afterward we brought the keys to the person responsible for them.

"I can't believe how quick this condo was sold. Maybe you should get into building them." "I would need a few millions for that, which I don't have and besides, the risk is much higher." "You must be right and besides, the houses you're building are so much nicer." "You think so, really?" "Yes, ours will be so beautiful. I can't wait to live in it." "It will come. I will begin the excavation next week sometime." "But the ground must still be frozen." "The ground is defrosting as we speak where the house will be built." "Already? You must be working even in your dreams?" "It's in my dreams that I find my directions." "What do you mean by that?" "I'm telling you that God is talking to me and guiding me through my dreams." "You're inventing this." "Not at all, what if I tell you that I learned to play the fiddle in my dreams, that I composed many, many songs where the ideas came from my dreams, that my ideas for my books came from my dreams, that I have ten very good inventions that came from dreams, that I found out the identity of the Antichrist from a dream and that I even learned to dance the cha-cha from a dream. I woke up in the middle of a night once and I was all in tears.

In that dream I was singing and living through a terrible nightmare." "What was the dream all about? I was singing my story and if you want to I'll sing it to you." "I would love that." "It's called; I'm Always upset and it goes like this;

I'm always upset.

I'm always upset. I'll never forget what happened to me that night.

I took one more drink, one more than I can take, to keep eyes opened I had to fight.

When soon on my way, it's not easy to say, I hit somebody on the road.

I jumped out my car. I could see that far, what happened was real and my fault.

There was on the ground dying when I found a girl looking like my daughter.

When she looked at me, she said as you can see I'm out of service forever.

She's sixteen years old and she was beautiful before she got hurt and fell down

She said; it's not fair. I don't have to be there, not more than my brother or sister.

Go find my papa and tell my mama, I was on my way to back home

I can remember when I told her mother what it was very hard to do.

I opened the door, she saw I was sore. She knew that I had a bad news.

And then she told me after hearing the story and I had to believe the truth

When two years ago I left home to go, she could not stay and ran away too.

She went everywhere, she looked here and there."

"Stop James. Stop, this is too sad. More than that, it could very well have been my own story. I just had better luck than that girl. I managed to bring my father home without any accident." "I'm so sorry my sweetheart. The last thing I would want to do is to make you cry." "It's not your fault, you had no way to know what happened in my childhood and it's not something I like to talk about." "Please sweetheart, stop crying. I just can't stand it. Tears in your eyes are just like darts in my heart. I was crying too when I woke up in the middle of that night and I went to sit at my table to write the whole song, the same song I was singing in the dream. This was a story I have never heard of before and one that was never in my mind either. It's not easy to understand all this." "It's no wonder why you're so full of wisdom. You say that you found the identity of the Antichrist and of the beast?" "The name of my second book is; The True Face Of The Antichrist, written following up a five thousand hours study of the Bible. The Antichrist himself challenged the world for the last two thousand years to discover his name, or the name of the beast that he crated, he said his number is 666." "But what is his name?" "Forgive me Janene, but I'm not ready to reveal it to the world just yet, the time is not yet come and don't forget the day it will be known, the beast will roar with rage and many disciples like us will be murdered. The day I will reveal it is the day that I'll sign my death certificate unless I have a lot of money to hide. I'm not really in a hurry for that. This beast always has been cruel and murderess." "All this is really scary." "But Jesus gave us a real good message on that subject in Matthew 10, 28;" "Don't fear the one who can kill the body but cannot kill the soul, but fear the one who can destroy the body and the soul in hell." "I love the word of God, it is instructive, it is comforting and it is full of life. I don't understand why so many people read it without following it." "No one can say that you don't following it." "I love walking with God. Talking about God's will, when do you think you're going to start making babies?" "I will as soon as you want to my dear love. What if we start that right away?" "Do you mean you're ready to give it a shot?" "I worked a lot of hours today, better take a bath first." "Don't forget that I have to pick up Danielle at eleven thirty." "That's true, better go right away, there is not that much time left." "We have two hours in front of us, that should be enough to make you happy and a nice looking baby." "You always make me happy James, it's so good to be with you. Sex must be the best thing God has made." "His will to fill up the earth would have never been fulfilled if He didn't make sex that good."

I think it was that particular night according to my calculations that my second son Jonathan was conceived. I was on time to pick Danielle up after work anyway. Among many others that day was quite special in our lives.

A week later I was just beginning to get use to my new machine, my new backhoe. I managed to get three feet deep before I was stop by the frost again. In a couple of days I'll be most likely under the frost and be ready to start the foundation. It's very important that the frost don't reach under otherwise it can break everything. Yes frost is stronger than concrete. One night taking Danielle after work like I did for the last ten days, she was in tears.

I don't think there is anything else that breaks my heart like this.

"But what is the matter for goodness sake?" "I made a mistake with the medicine and one of my patients is very sick because of me. She is so swollen, she's basically unrecognizable." "But you can't let that get to you like this, otherwise you wont be able to do your work anymore." "That is the first time it happened to me." "One mistake in eight or nine years, I don't think that is exaggerated." "In our position there is no room for mistake, people could die from it." "You are too hard on yourself, even doctors make mistakes. Which doctor was on calls tonight?" "It was Raymond, fortunately he knew the antidote. He said that she should be okay. I don't know if he reported me or not." "He won't miss such an opportunity for revenge." "It's true that it would be a great opportunity for him." "Let's go to bed anyway, there is no point pulling your hair off and yours is way too pretty anyway."

It took me a couple of hours, but I managed to comfort her. The next morning she asked me to take her with me to work insisting to know the basic of my trade.

"I don't go to the property today, because the ground is still frozen, although tomorrow if you still want it, I will go finish the excavation. Go back to bed and rest well. I'll wake you up tomorrow morning."

She went back to bed and I went to my jobs site. Raoul had everything under control and within ten days all the work in progress would be finished. There were three houses, but two of them were bringing me good profit when the third one barely brought me any. I thought that I will have to check that out to see what didn't work for that one. I just knew that there was something wrong somewhere.

"If you don't mind Raoul I would like you to finish the 222 and the 228 first. I don't see any problem with that and you surely have a special reason for asking." "Yes man, those two bring me a profit and the other one for a reason that I don't know yet doesn't bring me any." "That is very strange, isn't it? You made the estimations of all the three houses, didn't you?" "Yes and that is why I'm concerned, but I will find the cause, don't you worry. Alright I want you all at my farm in ten days, you know the directions, don't you? " "Yes, you gave them to me the other day." "That's all I had to say, do you have any questions?" "No, I think we have everything we need for now." "That's good and you call me if you need anything."

I then went home to find Danielle setting up the table and the meal was ready to be served. I don't think there is anything more enjoyable than to see the woman you love pregnant serving you a meal. I felt so much love for her at that precise moment that I had a hard time holding back my tears. I thank God every day that He brings me for my two loves of my life and for the joy that they give me.

"Hi darling, how are you doing?" "I'm fine thanks to you." "I'm fine too because of you. We're even." "You've received a few letters and I put them on your desk." "Thank you, I'll look at them after diner. Did I have any phone calls?" "No they let me sleep like an angel." "But you are an angel, my angel." "Only for you!" "Then I don't mind to be a bit selfish and keep you for myself." "Don't worry, I'm yours and I belong to you only. You're such a charming lady, no wonder I love you so much. Give me a kiss, that's all I want for dessert." "That's all I want too. I don't want to gain too much weigh."

After diner I went to open my mail. There was a letter from the provincial court and another one confirming the registration of our new property in the name of Janene, Danielle and myself. The letter from the court kind of forcing me to show up in court of Her Majesty the Queen at the indicated address on March the thirty first at ten o'clock a. m to testify at the trial of M Bernard Sinclair. I wondered who could have cited me as a witness. I certainly don't think it is one of the Sinclairs. It's got to be one of the doormen who wanted to prove that he had a good reason to throw Sinclair out of the building. But, why me? There were dozen of people who could testify of that. Finally I told myself that there was no point questioning, that I will find out soon enough. Janene could have been called as a witness too, but neither me nor herself was there when Sinclair came back armed with a loaded pistol. In fact there was no reason for neither of us to be call as a witness for a crime that we didn't witnessed. I had to show up in court anyway if I didn't want to be charged for a crime against Her Majesty the Queen. In the mean time life goes on. The next morning Danielle came with me to the property and I got her to join me inside the backhoe. So I continued digging while she was with me. I was happy to find out that the ground was rather dry. The necessary building material was delivered the day before. I spread out a good layer of crushed rocks which is good to avoid ground movements under the foundation. Everything that we needed was there, the re-bar, the concrete forms, the draining pipe, which is very important to get rid of the overflow waters, the sticky blue sealant that makes the foundation as waterproof as a swimming pool, the stir foam that keeps the cement from freezing. Of course Danielle wanted to learn and to know everything on the first day. She certainly wasn't made for this kind of work her who is so delicate and feminine. Tomorrow I will have to bring a helper who is capable to pound nails and wood stakes in the ground. Then I had to bring Danielle back so she could get ready for work. I certainly didn't like her situation at the hospital these days, but it was another week since we had another problem. The next day I finished the first part of the foundation with my transit and my new helper and at the end of the day we were ready to receive the cement. I got to say that I found a new way to pour the cement all in one shot, meaning footings and walls. When it's done all in one shot, it's way more waterproof. I make the foundation four and a half feet high to bring it two inches higher than the ground, which is cheaper and gives me a house a lot more heat efficient. I build up the rest of the foundation with two by eight so this way I can put in a good quantity of insulation and big size windows in which I can slide full sheets of plywood or drywall. Believe me it's worth it. It's also a good advantage if you ever want to rent the basement. The next day we had a very nice eight degrees which was perfect for pouring the cement. Most of the foundation workers line up the outside of the building, but I do it inside so this way I almost have a finished basement, meaning that I only have to put the stir foam on the walls and strap it with one by three every sixteen inches before the cement gets really hard. The spikes get into the cement then like it would in the soft wood and when the cement is hard there is no way you could pull these nails out. There you are with this trade trick you just can save quite a few thousands dollars and a lot of space and all of that very easily. We were done pouring by noon, which set me free for the rest of the day. I will have to come back in a couple of days to take off the forms. I brought my helper to the other site and then I went home. I was anxious to find out if my neighbours' properties were for sale as well and of course I wanted to buy before those two gain to much value. There was a lot of wood on them that I was interested in.

"Hi, is this M Fillion?" "Yes it's me, what can I do for you?" "It's me James. How are you M Fillion?" "James who?" "James Prince of course! Have you forgotten me already?" "No I didn't forget you, but I have a hard time recognizing voices on the phone." "It's understandable at your age." "Is there any problems?" "Not at all, but I can use some information." "If I can help you, I will." "I would like to know the names of my two neighbours, is that possible?" "Of course it is. The name of the one on the right side is Jean St Amant and the one on the left is Maurice Doiron." "Do you know where they live by any chance?" "Yes, they both live in Trois Rivières." "Did you spend all of your money already?" "No, but I have a hell of a nice forty-eight inches TV though." "That's good, take advantage of it. You know very well that we can't bring our money to the ground with us. Well, that's it for me, you've been very helpful and I thank you very much." "I'm glad to be able to help you James." "Take good care of yourself and see you soon."

It was almost time to take Danielle to work, but to free me some time she suggested that she travel by herself from now on.

"Don't even mention it, for as long as Bernard Sinclair is not behind bars. There are only a few days before the trial, so be patient, would you?" "But you could accomplish so much more if you didn't have to watch over me." "But I love to spend those extra twenty minutes with you."

That put an end to that discussion. Four days later it was the Sinclair's trial finally. I was there on time at the address of the invitation. Bernard Sinclair was already in the prisoner's box and the procedures had already started when my eyes stop on a different face that was not unknown to me, but was intriguing me a lot. The buyer of the condo agent was there present. I wondered about what would concern him enough to come and spend time in the court house, knowing how busy and always in a hurry he is. Then came the moment where I was called to sit on the witness seat and an officer came close by and asked me to put my hand on the bible.

"I don't swear sir." "You have to swear M Prince." "No sir, I can not be forced to swear."

"M Prince, would you tell the court why you don't want to swear?" "Yes your honour, I can tell you, but better yet if you allow it, I would like your officer to read the reason there in the bible. If he wants to open this same bible in Matthew 5 from 34 to 37 and read what is written." "Go ahead officer, please read what it is written in there."

"But I tell you not to swear at all, not by heaven, because it's God's throne, not by the earth, because it's his footstool, neither by Jerusalem, because it is the city of the great king, neither should you swear by your head, because you cannot make you hair black or white. Let your word be yes, yes and no be no, for what so ever is beyond that is coming from evil." "Officer, ask the man to promise instead than swear, would you please?"

"You understand M Prince that you could be charged for perjury the same way if you get caught lying to the court, don't you?" "I'm aware of that your honour."

"M Prince, do you promise to tell the truth, the whole truth and nothing but the truth? Lift the right hand and say; I promise." "I promise."

"Who said all this in the bible?" "He was the Christ himself, your honour. As far as I am concern, the courts and all the governments are Antichrist your honour." "Keep quiet M Prince." "But your honour, he made me promise to tell the whole truth." "If you don't keep quiet M Prince you will be charged with contempt of court."

"Can you tell the court M Prince what happen at or around twelve thirty in the morning the night of the thirteen of March of the year of two thousand and eight at the dance club; Le Tourbillon?"

"Answer the question M Prince." "But now I don't understand anymore, you made me promise to tell the whole truth and after I barely started I'm told to shut up, I decided then to shut up and you forcing me to speak for an answer. At twelve thirty that night I was with my fiancée at her apartment having the best snack of my life for my birthday." "I've heard enough of this. Please officer, set this man free to go and call in the next witness."

Then I stepped down the swearing box and a woman came to take the seat I was on. The same process continued and the woman on the stage told the court that she was confused and didn't know if she should swear or not. The judge then asked her to make up her mind and decide one way or the other. She and more than fifty per cent of the witnesses decided to promise rather than to swear. I couldn't help thinking about another message from Jesus in Matthew 10, 18;" "You will be brought before governors and kings to be witnesses to them and to the gentiles, because of me."

The judge declared the defendant guilty as charged and sentenced him to two years less one day to a minimal security mainly because he had no record of violence prier to that crime. It was at that moment that I found out what M Charron's agent was doing at the court house when he said to Sinclair that he was lucky that the law found him before he did. I found out later on that Bernard forced the door of the condo thinking it still belonged to my women. What Bernard didn't know is the new owner had the experts to install cameras inside and outside. But the biggest surprise came when the judge stood up and said that this was his last trial, that he would never be accused to be an Antichrist again. He then asked for a replacement judge on the spot. He gave me a very sad look and left the room. Another thing that surprised me a bit is the fact that the doctor wasn't there for his brother's trial. He must have known that his brother was in deep shit because of him.

Three days later Danielle made the same mistake again, but this time she was reprimanded by the director who didn't think it was funny at all. There is always the risk to be sued by the patient. One more time Danielle was devastated and didn't know what was going on. She even asked herself if it was because she was pregnant.

"If this happen to me again I will be suspended." "Of course not, they are too short of nurses in Quebec for that to happen, even temporarily. They're going to put you on surveillance before anything else. Right now they're asking retired nurses to come back to work. Why don't you ask to be on the same shift than Janene?" "This is a brilliant of a good idea. I have the impression that I'm going to need her. I'll see what they say about it. It's a good thing I've got you."

I don't know exactly why, but for some reasons I had doubts about her guilt in this whole affair as if all of the sudden Danielle was not a responsible person anymore. It just didn't make any sense. There is when I made a plan to discover the real guilty party. Of course I had my doubts when it comes to Doctor Sinclair, but I needed some proofs and there was no time to waste. I couldn't talk to Danielle about it either, because she could give me away with only one word at the wrong time. I found it hard to keep the secret from her, but I knew it was necessary. I called a friend of mine, a P.I, private investigator. The doctor didn't have too many friends, but he was going to make one that he won't forget too soon.

"Roger, I need you for a special and urgent cause that concerns me a lot." "You sound very concerned." "Yes, I am very disparate right now. I need you for a week or two. Are you busy?" "No, this is a good timing, it's pretty quiet right now and I'll be able to give you a good deal. What's the problem? What can I do for you?" "I need you to make yourself a new friend." "You know me James and you know that I choose my friends very carefully." "This one would be an exception and I choose him for you." "Who is he?" "It's Doctor Raymond Sinclair." "What do you think he's done?" "I think he has manipulated the medicine and he let Danielle take the blame for it." "Tell me why would he do such a thing?" "It could be by jalousie or for revenge, that's what you need to find out and bring me proof of it. You cannot let him have a clue that the investigation is going on otherwise it would be a complete failure, that's why I need your help. He eats every day at the restaurant a cross the street from the hospital." "What do you want me to do?" "I want you to become his friend and make him talk about it. I don't want to accuse him or getting charged or anything like that, I just want him to leave and give his resignation if he's guilty of course. You can choose your own methods, but I need a recorded confession." "Leave that with me, I'll take care of it as soon as tomorrow." "Roger, it's urgent." "Don't worry, I understood."

Now that Bernard Sinclair was behind bars, there was one less threat to us and I could perform full days work again. The work was going pretty fast since I create a sort of competition among the workers. There were two teams, one on the left of my quarters and the other one on the right. I put the foreman on one side with two carpenters and one apprentice and I took the other side with one carpenter and one apprentice. Both teams were equipped with the same tools. I gave the instructions to everybody in a fair way specifying the strategic points.

"Where it takes two nails, I want two nails and where it takes three, I want three. I don't want any mistake anywhere and if you make one, you'll have to repair it before you go any farther. It won't pay to cheat to save time. I will inspect the work each day after five. When one team is ready to lift one wall, the other team will come to help right away. Any question? Every one is ready? Now, let's go to work then."

I could tell right from the beginning that every one of them wanted to win. Raoul with his men went on to Danielle side and I took Janene side with my two helpers. I also told Raoul to not hesitate to contact me if he needs to. In one single day all the walls were standing up. At four thirty I went on the other side to measure the openings just to make sure that they were right. I was quite please, because only one of them was too small. After verification on the blue print, we concluded the mistake was a reading one, so we fix the problem without any cost to the other team. These things happen, but Raoul was concerned anyway.

"How come you did just as much as we did with a man less? You didn't even seem to rush." "You just try to pound nails down while rushing. You would miss more often than if you take your time to do it right. The whole trick is in the way to proceed. First I have to tell you that two men working together at the end of the day have accomplished one and one half day and that two men working separately have accomplished two days work. I'm talking about two good workers in both cases, of course." "How can you explain that?" "There are different reasons. Sometimes one guy is in the other one's way, sometimes there is too much discussion between the two of them and sometimes one is waiting for the other one to move before he can do anything. I was just a young boy of thirteen years old when I learned about this. We were six teams working in the wood and I was teaming with my dad. Father was the foreman and he was gone out of our road a full day every week to measure all the other teams' wood from Friday noon to Saturday noon and yet, none of the other teams could beat us. Every one knew that my dad wasn't the hardest worker either. We didn't work any harder than the others, but kind of smarter. That is the reason why one house didn't bring me any profit. I was not there as much as I was in the other two. The difference is in the cost of labour. I don't want men to work harder, but only smarter." "You should teach me how." "It's simple Raoul, you just have to diversify the work. You pick the best man with measurement, who knows the reading of the plan right and he will supply all the others who will keep installing. What you did today is one guy picked up a 2x6 measured it and went to install it. Every one of you did the same thing. I saw you going, but I wanted to prove my point before I talk to you. On my side the saw didn't stop for almost five hours. The carpenter and I installed all day without worrying about the measurements and without touching the saw and a measuring tape.

The difference is that we save one man salary without working any harder than you guys. You know as well as I do that three hundred dollars a day is a lot of money at the end of the month." "I'm forced to admit that you're right, the result is there."

After supper that day I went to show Janene what we had done and she couldn't believe her own eyes.

"But all this is incredible, how do you do it? You must have a dozen workers at least?" "No, we are seven guys, but we work efficiently and also the erection of the walls is what is the most impressive. Nothing shows in the morning and at the end of the day you have a whole building to show up." "Danielle and I have to talk to you this weekend about the house. We want to be together and talk with cool head." "This sounds very serious." "It's nothing bad, don't worry, but we both think it's important." "The least I can say is that you can be intriguing." "This house is going to be magnificent James, I can't wait to live in it, but it's going to feel strange to live without Danielle, you know that we live together for more than ten years." "Yes I know, but it's not very far from one place to the other, you can visit as much as you wish." "I don't understand what's happening with her at work. As far as I know that never happened before." "Is Doctor Sinclair has been there long?" "About a year and a half!" "You have worked with him too, haven't you? How was he with you?" "He was rather gentle, but as you already know, he was after me." "Did he ever show any sign of violence or impatience?" "Not really, I made a mistake once with the medicine too, but he never said a word about it and there was no consequence." "Do you know if that happened to other nurses?" "Not that I heard of!" "It is kind of strange that these things happen only the most conscientious nurses of the hospital, isn't it?" "Well, we are two women deeply in love, anything can happen." "That could be one reason yes, but let's hope that nobody dies in the process." "There is nothing we can do to change the way we feel about you anymore." "This is not what I want to change, Janene, I love you both way too much for that." "And what about going home now and make love my favourite carpenter?" "I want you too sweetie." "Take your time and make it fast, would you?"

There are things and words that we never forget and some of the moments and memories that remain precious the whole life time and I have a lot of them. Eight day after my conversation with Roger I had a phone call from Him.

"Do you want to come and meet me at my place, I think I have what you needed." "Are you sure your place is the best place for us to meet? If the doctor ever sees you and I together or me near your place, the whole investigation would be compromised." "You're right, it's risky." "You just wait till he's at work and you come to my place. The girls here know nothing about this and it has to stay that way until we got him." "Can you tell me why?" "Yes, he is a very intelligent man and he could pick up a clue in one of their conversation and I cannot take that risk." "If I ever need someone to help me investigate, I'll think of you." "Nevermind, I have enough to do with my flock."

The next day just before supper time Roger was at my house and I invited him to the basement after I introduced him to Janene who was preparing supper. I told Janene that we couldn't be disturbed under any circumstances for the next half hour and that it was very important. I listened very carefully to the tape and I understood that it wasn't quite enough to charge the doctor. The indisputable proof I was looking for was not on that tape.

"You've got to make him talk about the medicine more than this. He's got to say that he's the one who changed the prescription without telling Danielle. We know now that he did it, but I need a solid proof." "You realize that this will take more time and that Danielle is at risk to lose her job?" "Yes, but if we don't get a solid proof we are still a step behind and she could lose her job even more. Without a solid proof, he's the winner. So you keep going, would you? You are on the right track and you did well, but I need more." "It's hard to believe he can do such a thing, he's so gentle."

"That only proves one thing and that is that bad guys too can be gentle, but we still have to stop him. You going to stay with us for supper otherwise Janene would be insulted." "I wouldn't want to insult such a beautiful woman." "You can look, but you can't touch. For the details, you want to get a house built." "Understood ! " "One more thing before we go upstairs, you make it quick, invite him, make him drink, but make him talk the sooner the better." "I think he's got the weekend off." "That is the right time. Let's go."

We had a good supper and Roger had a very hard time to keep his eyes away from Janene, but I couldn't blame him because I told him that he could look. It's also true that she is the prettiest women I ever had the chance to meet. It took him three more days, but he came back with the necessary proof to put the doctor Sinclair ambitions away for a long time. The solid proof was directly from Raymond Sinclair's mouth recorded on tape as clean as a whistle.

"I had a hard time to believe my own ears James, he's such a kind man and so intelligent, but I don't think he wanted to do wrong." "Do you call that doing right to let someone else being accused for the thing you've done?" "But I think in the bottom of his heart he wanted to protect Danielle." "No matter what his motives are and no matter what he thinks, he caused us a lot of grief and his brother took two years in jail because of his ambitions, that too is not right." "Even so, I don't think he deserve jail time." "But I don't want to send him in jail, I only want him to stop causing us trouble and I wouldn't object if you want to be his friend. He really needs good friends, but I sincerely doubt that he could ever be part of my circle." "Can you leave me out of this from now on?" "No problem if this is what you want. How much do I owe you?" "With all of the expenses, you owe me two thousands dollars." "Do you think it was worth the cost?" "He was ruining Danielle's career and health, of course it's worth it. All I need to know now is where I can meet him to discuss with him without causing too much commotion." "At the restaurant where he goes for supper every night is a fairly quiet place. I have to tell you that he believes that you're cheating on Danielle with Janene and frankly, I don't think he's completely wrong." "I will inform you maybe one day, in the mean time I thank you very much, see you." "I wish I could say that I am proud to be any help to you, but I can't, sorry and good bye."

He was my friend, but not one whom I could confide to at that time especially not as far as my two women were concerned. The next day at seven thirty I was waiting at the restaurant where Doctor Sinclair usually takes his supper. I had with me a little tape recorder and the tape with the doctor's complete confession. I waited until he was almost finished and let me tell you that I didn't worry about him having an indigestion either. Then I got up and walked to his table allowing myself to sit down across the table in front of him.

"May I join you M Sinclair?" "Go ahead, don't be shy M Prince. You will understand that I don't have anything to say to you, but you certainly have a good reason to be here." "Good, because, I need you to listen and to listen very carefully." "Ho, that sounds very, very serious M Prince." "That will only depend on you Doctor." "So what can I help you with?" "On the contrary Doctor you will need to help yourself." "Me, but I don't need anything." "That's what you think, but I have in my pocket the proof that you need to find another job." "I don't want to go anywhere else M Prince, I'm just fine here surrounded by very capable nurses and gorgeous on top of all." "I've got something that you need to listen to Doctor." "What is it?" "Listen carefully, it's a short message that tells a long story." "Where did you get this?" "Where it's coming from is not important, what is important for you, for me and mainly for Danielle is that it is in my possession and that I wont hesitate at all to use it if necessary." "But this is blackmailing." "Call it the way you want it, but I have to protect the one I love and what you did to her is absolutely disgusting." "What do you want me to do?" "I want you to give your resignation immediately and clear Danielle of any wrong doing. In return I promise to never use this proof against you unless you force me to. Nobody else than you, me and the PI that I hired to make you talk knows any of this. By the way the private investigator is devastated about the whole thing and he thinks that you were doing this to help Danielle. Tell me why you changed the medicine?" "I was hoping she beg me to help her." "Contrary to what you seem to think Danielle and Janene are both very happy and satisfied. What you have done to your brother is also very disgusting and I'm sure that he needs you now. I saw him at his trial and he seemed to be lost." "Is there anything else?" "No, that's all, but I expect you to move on this as soon as tomorrow." "It would have been easy for you to send me to jail. I could be with my brother." "I couldn't do anymore for your brother and I'm sorry, because I don't think he deserves this and the province of Quebec needs too many doctors now days, even one like you is needed."

I took off and I was sure that he would move away, because he had no choice, it was that or the justice and his career. I went home to find Janene lonely, because she's not use to spend her evenings by herself anymore.

"How come you so late?" "I had to discuss with a client who had special restrictions." "I hope it doesn't happen too often, I missed you." "No, these cases are pretty rare, maybe one in a life time, at least I hope so. I'm tired, this guy has exasperated me." "I'm going to run you a hot bath that will do you good." "You're a sweetheart, just be sure that I appreciate it. If you want to I'll soap you, rinse you, dry you and after you'll see." "Anything you want darling."

I let her do everything she wanted, but the next day I wondered if I was drugged or not because, I could hardly remember anything that happen after that. Janene had to go get Danielle simply because she couldn't wake me up. Everything I had in the restaurant was before the doctor came in. I concluded then that it was only some accumulated fatigue. For the last couple of weeks I was going to bed late and getting up early so I didn't look any farther.

The time to shingle the house has come and if is there a place where you have to be awake among others is on the roof. My two loved nurses understood that it was time for them to give me a little break. They decided to give me a complete weekend off and did I sleep. At supper time the following Monday Danielle came up with the great news.

"James, I'm clean." "What do you mean, you're clean? You're always clean." "I mean that the director of the hospital apologized to me, because it was not my fault with the medicine, but doctor Sinclair's mistake. He admitted it and gave his resignation. He's no longer one of our staff." "Ho what a great news darling, though I confess to you that I didn't think you were guilty. You are so conscientious with everything you do. We have to celebrate this. What would you say If I open a bottle of champagne?" "Champagne? You're always ready for everything, aren't you?" "This is a great day, we have to celebrate this." "I'll be able to travel alone again now that Sinclair is no longer around. He said that he's got a job at the other end of the country." "I'll go to the basement and get a bottle and then we'll put some music on and dance until my legs give up. What do you think of that?" "It's magnificent my love."

Yes, it was a nice day and yes we have celebrated and yes we danced and yes we made love until we fell asleep. It was nice to come back to a peaceful and normal life again.

One day I received a strange letter from the penitentiary. It was from Bernard Sinclair who was asking me to pay him a visit. At first I thought of ignoring him completely and then I asked myself; what if it was me who was behind bars, wouldn't I want someone to pay me a visit from time to time? I knew my answer the day that I went.

"I was not expecting you anymore." "I wondered for a long time what possible business I could have with you and I told myself that I didn't need you and that I didn't want to have anything to do with you. Then I told myself that your brother was far away and that you might have nobody at all to pay you a visit. So here I am. What do you want from me?" "First I want to thank you for saving my idiot brother's butts, he probably didn't deserve your compassion. Then I finally realized that you could very easily demolish me the night at the club, but you didn't do it. I was at your mercy, but you didn't hit me even though I deserved it. And I also reflected at what you did at my trial where you have chosen not to testify against me, which could have been a lot more incriminating. And finally I've been wondering since then how you could convert a provincial court judge and more than half of the attendance like you did. There is something in your ways that is not natural. I would like you to tell me what it is." "If there is something special, I would say that it's because I walk with God and that God is with me." "That is exactly what I thought. You know when someone is in a place like this here, he's got a lot of time to think and to reflect about his life. I would like to walk with God too and when I'm out of here I would love you to show me how." "Why wait till you out of here?" "But there is nobody but criminals in here and most of them are pretty much set in." "There is no better place in the world to start a ministry than here." "You're joking!" "Not at all!" "But what can I do over here?" "Just be a blessing for everyone around you and you will receive a multitude of blessings from God, but don't expect anything. I will come back to see you and I will bring you a book that I like very much called: The True Face Of The Antichrist. You can learn just about everything that you need to know from it." "The visiting time is almost over and I had so many more questions for you." "Don't worry I'll be back."

"Over, visits are over."

"I'll be back." "Thanks for coming."

If I could ever expect such a thing to happen. It's true that it is written that the thoughts of God are precious and impenetrable. I went back a week later and I brought him a bible and the book that I mentioned to him. There was enough in that book to cause him death for the knowledge that he will acquire, but I warned him about it.

Chapter 5

The work in process with our house was going pretty good and one evening after supper I brought in this next question just to make sure that everything was alright with all of us.

"If one of us had a reproach to make to another one either small or big, what would it be?" "Do you really think this is necessary?" "Yes, I think that it would be better to talk about it than repressing the feelings even unconscientiously. I had a girlfriend who kept things to herself for six months and when she finally let it out I was totally stunned. I could not believe that a person could have such a grudge against you and keep kissing you. I'm telling you that my arms drop down and so did my hope for a happy life too, with her anyway. I could not accept the fact that she pretend to be happy while she wasn't. It was a lie, treason and that just can't be good for the relationship. I could never put my trust in her anymore and I left her so yes I think it is very important. I only have a small reproach for both of you, but I think it could have some very serious consequences." "Ho yeah and what is that?" "it's your lack of cautiousness! It's your turn now." "We both think that you were too hard on Tremblai, after all it was our decision to ask him to keep our contract in his office." "Ho, this is what you believe my dear ladies. Here is what I'm going to do for you. I will change the scenario to help you understand my point of view. I hope you would allow me." "Go ahead, we're listening." "Here we are. You just sold your condo and your furniture for three hundred thousand dollars and you go to M tremblai to complete the transaction. Here how it goes."

"Hi, can we speak to M Tremblai please?" "I'm sorry, but M Tremblai passed away that's a bit more than two months ago now. Is there anything I can do for you? My name is Alphonse Gagnon and I'm the one who took over M Tremblai's practice.

More than half of his files will be destroyed by the crown very shortly. Can you tell me your names?" "I'm Janene St Louis and this is my friend Danielle Brière." "Ho that's you. I was just getting ready to contact you for an eviction notice.

The condo was sold lately and the new owner wants to take possession of the apartment right away. Normally you can have thirty days notice, but in a case of a sale you would have to leave immediately. You only have two days to get out of there. So here is your notice and a list of the things you cannot take with you. You are allowed to take all of your personal belongings, but nothing else if you don't want any trouble with the justice." "But all of this is ours." "Do you have your contract?" "You know very well where our contract is, bastard." "Ho, here come the big words. Yes I have here the contract of this condo in the name of barrister Alfonse Gagnon and it was acquired in 1999 for the amount of one hundred and forty-nine thousand dollars. It's written black on white right here. If you need any references I can supply them to you since you always paid you rent on time and no one can blame you for anything, except big words. I like to thank you personally." "It wouldn't end here you dribbler, son.o.a.b." "Big words again, but I think that you are the ones who are dribbling right now."

"Your next appointment is with a different lawyer and one that you don't know, because the one you had trust in just passed away unfortunately. So you tell him all the facts to the best of your knowledge and here is his reaction."

"This is going to be a very long and expensive process. It's always the way when a lawman is involved. I will need ten thousands dollars to start with and there is no guarantee that I will succeed to recover your money."

"Now this lawyer already knows that it's a lost cause, but he's got in front of him two young women completely ignorant of the legal process and he's got to make a living anyway. Six months later you spent fifty thousands dollars and you're still at the same point, meaning a dead point. In the mean time the work on our beautiful house was suspended, because of a shortage of money. Your lover, the poor man did everything he could, but he ran out of money anyway. It was not a project that he could handle by himself. He mortgaged his house to the maximum possible, because he has to supply a shelter to his two loves of his life. Now he's facing bankruptcy and the risk of loosing everything is quite high. He put a lot of trust in his two partners, but they can't do anything to help him anymore. They are very desperate, but that doesn't change the facts. Now their beautiful dream is shattered. James was so confident that he invested everything he had in his new projects. He already bought the two neighbours properties, because he's got a great vision and he has at heart the privacy, the tranquility and peace for his family." "Stop right there James, that's enough. Stop this scenario before you leave us." "Do you still think that I was too hard on M Tremblai?" "No, but you're too hard on us." "Don't cry, but I hope that is a lesson you will remember for the rest of your live, because I might not always be there for you." "Do you think of leaving one day." "Certainly not voluntarily, but anything can happen. Jesus was only thirty-three when God came to get him." "Stop, you scaring us." "That said, I must leave you for a few days." "Can't we come with you?" "No, I have to be alone a little bit to collect myself." "Where are you going?" "I'm going to Winnipeg." "What are you going to do over there? You don't know anyone." "No, but they are exposing Louis Riel's poems and I want to see if I can find the proof of what I think, that he was a prophet. I wanted to clear the matter up for a long time. Those poems are a hundred and twenty-five years old and more." "I would love to come with you so much." "I'm sorry Danielle, but not now, maybe some other time." "Why do I have the impression that you're leaving us?" "Don't be stupid, I will never leave, but you must understand that I could use a break if it's not too much to ask." "You're right James and you deserve every bit of it. I'm going to use this time to visit my parents."

"And I'm going to be left here all by myself."

"Poor Janene, you just have to come with me, my parents will be glad to welcome you and we have so much to tell them." "We should take pictures of the house otherwise they wouldn't believe us. When are you leaving James?" "I'm leaving Friday and I'll be back Sunday night." "Then we have to take advantage of the time we have left." "Now I recognize you, we always have to take advantage of the time that we spent together. Sorry for being a bit rough on you earlier, but I want you to know that there are two legs rats with short tails in this world and they cause a lot more damage that the four legs ones with long tails." "We understood now James." "Do you have anything else to blame me for?" "Nevermind, we'll let you know as we go if you don't mind." "That's my girls. Well what about a few dances now to change our minds?" "That's a very good idea. It's a Samba." "No, it's a meringue." "You're right James."

"Hey, I want to dance too." "Come I love to do the mambo with you." "I'm so glad that you have invested in your legs." "It's a good investment, because we're going to benefit it for the rest of our lives. Did you think about a dance floor in your new place?" "You can bet that if we have enough money left, we both going to have one." "I save you more money with the finishing of your basement that it will cost for the dance floor, beside allowing you to get one hundred square feet more." "How did you do that?" "Simply by avoiding to build an extra wall inside the foundation." "I noticed that you left a foot with no stirfoam at one foot from the floor, can you tell me why?" "Sure I can, this is necessary for the cement not to crack and besides, it gives me the space that I need to run the plugs and the electric wires. Also at this particular place we don't really need insulation." "That is genial." "It comes only with experience." "To change the subject, you're not going to Winnipeg with your car, are you?" "Of course I'm going with my vehicle. I like it too much to leave it behind." "But you don't mind leaving us behind?" "Yes, but it's not the same thing." "No it's not, your car would miss you too much. You didn't want me to take my car to travel at four hundred miles from here in four days and you want to travel three thousand miles in three days." "Yes but for me it's not the same, I'm a man." "If you go with your car, I'm going with you, you will need an extra driver."

"I'm going too, because you'll need two extra drivers." "Don't you realize that I'm pulling your legs off." "You're pulling our legs and you think you're funny." "No, I'm taking the plane Friday morning and I already have a rented car waiting for me at the airport." "But this is really expensive isn't it?" "No, not for me." "Stop pulling our legs, would you? It becomes annoying." "I'm not pulling anything, did you feel something? I have accumulated enough air miles for the trip, that's all." "Ho, that's what it is." "Janene and I are going to enrich the poor gas companies and the poor government by traveling by car to visit my family." "Be careful traveling on this road, there are some storms even in May sometimes. Check with the forecast before you hit the road too." "We will, don't worry." "You be careful too and be good." "Me being good, but girls, you already know that I'm full of wisdom, don't you?" "Yea, yea, we know."

"No but seriously, this is the first time that you're going away and frankly we don't like it that much." "This is only for a few days and we will come out of this stronger." " Ho, you must be right again." "Ho yea that is not very funny, isn't it? I know, I hate to always be right, but I cannot be wrong just to please you, can I? There is no way out. Alright I'm going to bed, which one is taking me tonight?" "It's mine turn."

"No, it's mine." "I'm telling you that it is my turn." "I'm telling you too that it's my turn."

"Come on, who did I sleep with last?" "We can't remember." "Come on, you cannot forget something like that." "About you Janene, do you remember?" "Give me a second here to think about it."

"Nevermind, you're pulling my leg! Ha, ha, ha! Let's go Danielle. Good night any way Janene." "Good night James and let me kiss and hug you. Good night Danielle."

"Good night Janene and sleep well to be in good shape, because tomorrow night it will really be your turn." "Don't worry, I'll give him enough for the three days that he'll be gone." "So I should leave him enough for you." "That's nice, thank you."

When Friday morning came I was like I should at the airport an hour earlier than my departure. I didn't have too much luggage, because I was only going for a few days. All I took with me is a shaving kit and a bag with underwear, socks and a few shirts plus my briefcase. I had a problem going through the metal detector, because of a little negligence from my part. I passed through once and I was told to take my belt off because of the buckle. When I passed through the second time they asked me to put my arms up.

"What's going on?" "Keep your arms up sir." "What is going on? I'm not a criminal." "Do you have a weapon sir?" "A weapon, of course not!" "Keep your arms up sir, don't force us to shoot you."

Then I remembered that nowadays the police officers seem to have a light trigger finger and they don't mind using their laser gun which have killed many people by now. So I calmed down and I let these people do their job, which was to my advantage anyway. Then a woman police officer approached me carefully pointing a gun towards me like many other one and she put her hand in my right side pocket and pulled out three spikes.

"You must follow us sir." "Listen this is an innocent mistake, I'm a carpenter." "What do you want to build on the plane sir?" "I took my wife to be to our new house in construction last Sunday morning and I picked those three nails up to save tires and I totally forget about them, that's all."

Then another policeman entered the room with document in hands.

"You are M James Prince, president of Fiab Construction Enterprises of Trois Rivières?" "Yes sir!" "You have no criminal record." "My record is clean sir." "Alright you can go, but just be more careful next time." "I'll try to never forget what happened here today sir."

Of course it was an innocent mistake, but it was one that could have turned to a tragedy. The rest of the trip was fine, but that was a rather sour start. I managed to read many poems, but I didn't really find what I was looking for except the fact that Riel said he wasn't scare to die, him who was still young and had a wife and children. That in itself demonstrated that he was in peace with God and with himself a bit like the Jews when they were facing death at the holocaust and Stephen at his stoning. I also took advantage of this trip to visit Louis Riel own house that he had in St Vital and I have to admit that it felt strange. Vital was my grand father first name. I felt a sort of uneasy feeling and a sort of well-being feeling at the same time, I couldn't really explain it, maybe his spirit is still around, who knows?

On Sunday night at eight I was back home. I found my house quite empty, because my dear ladies weren't back from their trip yet. Danielle's parents are living only a couple of hundred miles away, but I know that anything can happen on the road. Nevertheless it was still too early to start worrying about it. It was a bit different though when they weren't in pass midnight. So I decided to call M Brière, even if it was late in the night to find out if he knew about where they may be. He reinsured me when he said that they left late and that they should be in by one thirty. I thanked him and I apologized for calling so late in the night.

Alright, I told myself, it is time to prepare their return properly. I set up the table and I got the candles out. I also prepared a little snack and I put in front of their plates a little present that I bought in Winnipeg. I then turn off the lights and I went to lie down while waiting for them to come in. As soon as I heard their car come in I got up and I light up the candles and I went back to lie down again.

"Don't make any noise Janene, he must be sleeping and you know how much he needs his sleep." "He works so hard and it's true that we take a lot of sleep away from him." "Hay look, he brought us something."

I got up making sure that they couldn't hear me and I went to watch them from a distance.

"Do you think we should open them?" "Yes, he put our name on them." "He's not sleeping for long the candles are hardly melted." "You go first Janene, this looks like a diamond ring's box."

"Do you really think so?" "Come on open it up, aren't you curious? Here take this knife to cut the tape." "It's crazy, but I'm a little scared." "Don't be foolish Janene there is nothing bad coming from him." "Ho, ho, ho!"

Janene burst into tears and I quickly came out of my hiding.

"I never really officially ask you to become my wife and I thought it was over due to do it. What is your answer?" "Yes, yes, yes, yes, yes, yes! I love you so much. I'll be for you the perfect wife." "But you already are sweetheart." "It must have cost you a fortune? It looks like real diamonds." "It's not polite to ask the price of a gift, but they look good on you so don't question anymore."

"What is the matter with you Danielle, you're not curious?" "I just want to congratulate Janene before I open mine."

"Come here Janene, I'm so glad that you are my friend."

"And you James, you will never stop surprising us, will you?" "Come on, go open yours now, I can't wait to see your reaction." "It's a blouse. Gosh it's the nicest I ever saw. Thank you darling it is wonderful. Let me kiss you." "Danielle, I would like you to try it now." "Ho that can wait till tomorrow." "Please Danielle, try it okay?" "It is late James, it was a long day and I'm tired and it can wait till tomorrow." "I'll help you, just take your sweater off." "James, please?" "This wouldn't even take a minute. I'm just curious to see how it fits you." "Alright, gees you can be a bugger when you want to." "It fits you wonderfully." "Something is scratching me in there though." "I wonder what that can be. Take it off and take a look." "That must be some needles to hold the pleat together. James, why are you doing things like that?" "Because I love you with all of my heart my love."

That's what I told her getting on my knees at her feet. I had hided the diamond necklace with the ring and the bracelet in the shoulders of the blouse.

"Would you marry me the sooner the better my love?" "I'll marry you tonight, tomorrow and every time that is my turn, my love."

"Hey, me too."

"I hope you didn't think that I was going to ask one to marry me and not the other." "No, you basically asked me to marry you the first night we met." "Ho yea!" "Don't you ever do something like that again." "There is no chance. I don't plan to ask you another time. Take me to bed and marry me."

"Good night Janene." "Good night both of you."

"How did the trip go?" "Good, but if you allow me Danielle will talk about it tomorrow, because tonight I need an affectionate lover not a questioning one." "Come here and let me love you then."

It was one thirty in the afternoon before I felt like going to work. Raoul already knew that I could be late. The roof was almost ready to receive the shingles and then it will be time to install the windows also. My little lesson at the beginning worked well, because we were two weeks ahead on our predictions. There were two or three more projects that I couldn't wait to start also at that time. The main one was my marriage with Danielle and for this all we were waiting for was for the house to be completed. Then I couldn't wait to get on my backhoe to clear the roads all around the property. The third but not the least was the stock breeding a dear project of mine. I didn't really have to, but I preferred to talk and discuss the matter with my two beautiful spouses.

"Sweethearts, I need to talk to you about my new project tonight." "Tell us, what is it?" "To start with I have to tell you that the house will be ready on time and maybe a bit sooner." "Is that mean we're going to have enough money?" "It means more than that, it means that you wouldn't have to use the money that you borrowed from the bank, so you can go pick your furniture as soon as you feel like it." "Are you sure of that?" "Of course I'm sure of that. Now I would like to talk to you about my breeding project that I mentioned to you once." "You never said that you wanted to breed animals. You're talking about animals, don't you?"

"Of course I want to raise a family or two too, but here right now I'm talking about breeding and training dogs." "Dogs? But what kind of dogs?" "I want some Mutesheps." "What kind of dogs are they, I never heard of them, in fact I never heard even this name." "That is because they don't exist for very long. It's a mix of Malamute and German shepherd. I have a friend in the West end of the country who created this new breed. I met him a few years ago. He had his problems with the Kelowna S.P.C.A in British Colombia. I was quite impressed with a phrase he told one journalist that I was lucky to read." "What was this phrase that touched you so much?" "He said; when we are persecuted in one town we have to flee to another, but because I am persecuted by the province, I have to flee to another." "It's normal to flee somewhere else when we are persecuted. There is nothing so strange in this. What made you want to meet him?" "This phrase is from Jesus and to my knowledge there is not that many people who follows his instructions. I knew then that this man was a Jesus' disciple. I learn a lot of things from this man. I can even tell you that this man put me on the trail of the Antichrist. He also made a song on the S.P.C.A about his dogs. Every once in a while I go on his Website to listen to it and it touches me every time." "What is his Website address?" "It's; www. hubcap.bc.ca. He also owns what is believed to be the largest hubcap collection in Canada." "Interesting, but why his dogs?" "They got something special. You can also see them on his Website. You can read a part of his book too. In fact he looks a lot like me in many ways and that is probably why I'm interested in this man. But let's come back to our business here, that's not all I want to raise. I want to raise pigs and rabbits also." "Pigs? Don't you realize that it will stink awfully?" "Not if I put them where I'm thinking of." "But why pigs? You don't even eat pork." "But you know why I don't eat it, don't you?" "Yes, you told us that you think that pork could cause cancer." "And why did I tell you this?" "Because God forbidden it to his children." "You cannot deny that there are a lot of cancer cases in the world now days." "So why do you want to raise them then?" "I need to prove to the whole world that God had a good reason to forbid it." "Don't tell us that you're going to give us cancer to prove your point." "Are you nuts? I want to feed my dogs with pork and rabbit. Yes I'm going to raise rabbit too and make a dog and catfood with pork and rabbit. Both of them are forbidden meat from God, and I strongly believe that God has a real good reason to do this. You see, we know for sure that cancer is cause by parasites and we also know that pigs are full of them. I don't really know if rabbit is full of parasites too, but I know that God forbid it and that is enough for me. Parasites, do you know what that is?" "Yes, they are little worms, aren't they?" "You're right and either you cook the worms or not, it is still vermin. Do you know what the pig's surname is?" "Not really!" "It's call a boar which is verrat in French and it means ver for worm and rat for rat. Now we know that pork is extra fat and that rabbit is extra lean, which will give me a very well balanced dogfood and besides, it will be all natural. If I'm mistaking it will be okay too, because I will have a good business and dogs and cats will be well fed and if I'm right then I'll have the necessary proof that I need to alert the world population." "Where in the bible did you find this?" "That is in Isaiah 65, 4 and 66, 17. The whole warning is also in Leviticus 11, 6-8; "The rabbit also, for though it chews cud, it does not divide the hoof, it is unclean to you, and the pig, for though it divides the hoof, thus making a split hoof, it does not chew cud, it is unclean to you. You shall not eat of their flesh nor touch their carcasses; they are unclean to you." Do you know that I can't find beef sausages in the stores that are not wrapped in pork skin? I also have to go to many restaurants before I can find beef sausages or turkey bacon to eat with my eggs. This is not too inviting for the children of God for breakfast in restaurants. I'm glad I finally found turkey bacon in the store. I often gave my pork bacon to my dog." "The only thing that bothers me is the smell of the pig's shit." "You will smell nothing at all or next to nothing unless you come directly in the pigsty." "How would you do that?" "As you know now I bought both of our neighbours and as you know too the wind almost always blows from North to South and from West to east and besides, I will have a very well kept pigsty. And if I can't eliminate the smell completely I'll move the pigs somewhere else." "So we are not at risk at all." "That might not be completely true." "What do you mean?"

"Well all this is a very huge project and I was hoping that you lend me the money that you have borrowed from the bank.

I could pay you a ten per cent interest." "I think I have a better idea than that." "If it's better I will certainly consider it." "What would you say If I invest that money in your enterprise?" "I'd say that would be splendid, awesome, but are you sure you want to do this?" "If you want to invest in this business it's because you think it's good so yes I want to invest with you."

"Me too, take me with you and I don't care if I lose everything." "Well I didn't really expect this outcome. Don't worry Janene, you wouldn't lose anything, I've been giving this project careful considerations for quite some time now. How much do you want to put in?" "I will put in the whole loan amount, the one hundred thousand dollars."

"Me too!" "Then I will give you both twenty-five per cent of the shares." "If you think this is fair we agree." "This is not all, with the rabbit fur I will make some jackets, some coats, some slippers, some mitts, some bedspreads and mainly some sleeping bags. The rabbit fur is one of the most thermal of all. Of course we'll have a tannery too. I need money to start with to build the slaughterhouse, the pigsty and the tannery and also for the fence. This fence has to be put two feet deep in the ground and stand up eight feet high so we don't lose our rabbits even in the winter. We will need approximately fourteen hundred lineal feet of fence. The brushwood is very important to protect the newborns from the daddies who don't want any competition. All the branches piles are good for that as well. They will have the water that they need in the summer and in winter they can eat the snow like every other wild animal in the country. If I start with two males and twenty females now, we will have one hundred thousands rabbits in eighteen months which will be worth around one million dollars." "Come on, you are pulling our legs again." "No, I'm taking you for a ride and it's quite a ride, you'll see. The rabbits will attract the wolves, the coyotes and the fox from everywhere around and I intend to ask for a trapping license for my properties which shouldn't be too hard to obtain. That should bring another twenty to forty thousands a year. I actually invented a big cage to trap them." "Don't you think that those wolves will be dangerous for us and the kids?" "No, they won't be able to come in because of the fence and they will die trying. But first I will find out if there is a market for their fur and also find out if their meat is eatable. I don't see why not since the Japanese eat dogs I don't see why dogs cannot eat wolves. Although, I'll have to go get the rabbits in Alberta." "Why so far? It's got to be a lot of rabbits around here." "Yes there are a lot of rabbits around here, but they are small like four to five pounds. I saw some in Alberta that are from eight to twenty pounds and they are the ones I want to breed." "What do you want to do beside all this?"

"Come on Danielle, don't you think this is enough now? We'll never see him." "There is a lot more I want to do, but don't you worry I love working, but I'm not workaholic." "But what else do you plan to do?" "I would like to make a plantation on each of the two farms I bought beside our property. If I plant a pine tree or a cedar now in twenty years from now it will be worth twenty dollars at least so if I plant one hundred thousands of them I'll get two millions and in the mean time we can use the wood. That would certainly be a nice gift to leave to our children." "The least we can say about you is that you think ahead and see far away. When in the world did you get the time to think about all this?" "I didn't have to rack my brains about all this it simply comes in my dreams.

If my father would listen to my mom he wouldn't have to wait for his pension cheque to eat when he's retired. I just don't know if this is still possible, but it was a time when the government actually gave the trees and loan the tree planting machine. Mom bugged my dad to do it, but my dad never consented. They really had a nice place for that as well." "Did you ever thought of becoming a politician?" "I thought of it, but I love my freedom way too much for that and besides, I would be impossible to be a politician and also make your happiness. An another thing too, I cannot be a politician without being an Antichrist, because they all have to swear on the bible and that is Antichrist, see Matthew 5, 34-37." "That's true too, forget about politics, I rather have the pigs and keep you at home with us."

"It doesn't mean that I cannot have an opinion on the matters." "What do you think of Obama?" "I think that he's very intelligent and a real diplomat." "What make you say that?" "When he came to Canada for the first time he took it by the tail of a……..beaver." "What do you think of the Bloc Quebecois and the péquistes? " "The name says it all, they will end up causing a lot of quarrels in the province, it's unavoidable, because it is one half of the population that wants to remove the other half. That is what the separation would do. It cannot happen without any hitch. These couple of last sentences will make me a lot of enemies, but I already have more than half of the world population as enemy, because of the word of God. Jesus said that I will be hated by all because of his name. If things go the way I see them we'll have one store or more in every large city in Canada and also in most of the medium towns also. We will do like most of the big store chains meaning rather than to pay too much income taxes we will open more and more stores. The world is big, but this is enough talking for tonight we got to sleep, because tomorrow we got to start working on all this." "When do you plan to begin all this?" "As soon as our house will be finished."

As usual I put them both to sleep my own way and the next day I was on the roof of our house with the other workers. There again I divided the work in even parts for everybody. I was completely done on my side when Raoul was hardly half way done on his side.

"You didn't already finish your side, did you? " "Yes we did." "How could you? Are you a sort of magician or something like that?" "A magician wouldn't have half of what you've done, but you are traveling from left to right while I install shingles. Come with me on the other side of your roof and I'll show you how. You make four lines from the top to the bottom right in the middle at one shingle distance then you install shingles from the bottom to the top following these lines and all the rest will be straight. Then you put one guy on each side and if you have a left handed and a right handed that will be better yet. Don't forget to put the bundle of shingles near you so this way you stop traveling. Now if you do this you're going to save me money without working harder or faster. I easily install seven bundles an hour. You install three and you costing money when you supposed to make me money." "I have to admit that we learn a lot with you." "Yea, you will probably be my competition before long." "It's not really my intention you know, when a man is treated well and he's happy, he doesn't look anywhere else." "That's good then, let's cover this roof before we get rained on."

From one thing to another we were already close to the summer vacation near the last two weeks of July and the house was almost completed. There were just a few minor things left to do. In the mean time I had paid Bernard Sinclair a few visits as well, this man became a devoted Jesus' disciple inside the jail. I couldn't believe my own ears when he told me that more than half of the prisoners became his fans and that the guardians could for the first time of their history take an afternoon coffee break. The most rebellious among them didn't like that that much, but didn't dare intervene. Another one who didn't like it at all was the penitentiary chaplain who couldn't understand what was going on. The result was a good saving for the government, because many prisoners were released sooner for their good behaviour. I was laughing to myself thinking that maybe I should send a bill to the government. I was quite happy to hear this news and I was glad to see Bernard happy as well. I reminded him not to forget his brother in this race for the conquests, that he might be his only chance. He made a funny face, but admited that I might be right. He might have known by then that a prophet or a disciple is not welcome in his own family.

Then the big, big day finally arrived. Danielle's flat was completed and it was there that we celebrated our marriage. We only had our close family and sure friends as guests. A magistrate for a decent price came to our place to celebrate the ceremony. Janene and Danielle synchronized their holidays with the construction holidays to allow us to leave all together for a well deserved vacation. Danielle couldn't really hide her pregnancy. It is true that she carries one part of me, but God do I find her extra pretty when she's pregnant.

My last employee, this young apprentice was not too enthusiastic about the forced vacations, because he didn't work for too long and he didn't have enough money to enjoy them. I offered him to work those two weeks on the road around the property consisting in cutting the good for nothing little trees and to replant the good ones in the field. I spent enough time with this young man to know that I could trust him. He also had to keep an eye on our house for the time we were gone. I also told him that he could swim and fish as much as he wanted, but that he has to save us a few trout and that I was not paying him for the time he was entertaining himself.

Danielle had already bought bran new and complete furniture that caught people eyes and made many of them envious. Janene bought hers too, but it wasn't home yet for the simple reason that her side wasn't quite finished yet. On Danielle side even the basement was all finished and we had the reception right there on a super nice hard wood floor. We had a lot of congratulations not only about the marriage but also about the house and it was quite flattering to hear them.

I made a little scenario for Janene to be included and be part of the ceremony. Here is how it went;

"Repeat after me. I Janene St Louis, I mean Danielle Brière." "I Danielle Brière." "Take you for my husband." "Take you for my husband." "James Prince here present." "James Prince here present." "To love and cherish." "To love and cherish." "For all the eternity!" "For all the eternity!" "I James Prince!" "I James Prince!" "Take you Janene St Louis, I mean Danielle Brière." "Take you Janene St Louis, I mean Danielle Brière." "To love and cherish." "To love and cherish." "For all the eternity!" "For all the eternity!" "I declare you husband and wife, you can kiss now and may God be with you."

There we were all married to one another almost without causing any suspicion. Only my sister Céline noticed the artfulness in the ceremony. The judge himself declared us married without making too many faces. Both my wives knew about the sincerity of my feelings and in the bottom of my heart I knew that I will be their husband for the rest of my life and beyond. I kissed Danielle the way I should and I also kissed Janene and thank her for her artful work.

I had rented out a full size motor home and we went towards Niagara Falls. I had also rented out a nice covered boat that contains everything a person could possibly need on Lake Erie. There is where we spent most of our holiday. After many calculations the difference between this and hotels weren't that much. This way everything was handy, but we had to help ourselves. We did just about everything; some fishing, some sun bathing, some swimming, some walking, some dancing, some boating of course, some movie watching, some sex and to tell you the truth that was a two weeks gone way too fast. Both of my wives were extremely happy just like me and wouldn't want to have it any other way. Everything was perfect. The whole trip was way too short and we promise ourselves to do it again every year. As far as work was concerned though, it was more than time for me to come back. I had men to put back to work and some customers to satisfy. It was time too to start the breeding business, which I had at heart. To start with I rented out a trencher to make a trench two feet deep by three inches wide all around the property. Then I slid some insulated boards which are twenty by sixty-four inches into the trench. Those boards are two inches thick and made out of insulation covered with galvanized sheet metal on both side. They actually came out of your metal entrance door, those pieces that were replaced by your door window. I can get them cheap, because they end up at the dump otherwise. But because they are solid and strong they are Ideal for my needs. I put them in the ground at twenty-four inches deep to stop the rabbits and the dogs to cross over the other side through a tunnel they could dig. This way they will get discouraged long before they could get through. That will also stop predators from coming in as well except in the place where I want them to come in.

My two ladies were following me every day, because they both had another week off. There is nothing like seniority. There is nothing either like questions to be informed except answers maybe and they had a lot of questions for me. We had fourteen hundred posts to put in the ground which is one at every ten feet, but that was quite easy, because I pound them down with the backhoe. Since we don't have a rocky ground it went very well. The whole place is also pretty well level which is a very good thing also. Of course we had to clear the road first and the brushwood and the branches didn't look to nice, but they were going to save a lot of little rabbits. I had spent enough time with Raoul by then too to let him take care of my construction sites which gave me a lot of time free. Everything went well and pretty soon I had both ends and the West side completely done. I would need a lot more hands to do the East side. When all the posts were in the ground and all the boards were installed and the whole fence was ready to install, I invited in twenty-five additional people to make a battue to bring in as many deer as possible and then lift up the whole fence all in one shot. I was hoping to get at least one buck and one doe. I knew that we could possibly bring some predators too, but I knew too that I could take care of them. The closest any wild animal could get to the house was four hundred feet. All along that fence I installed hundreds of eight inches solid plastic circles to trap the predators. I put some at two feet from the ground for the summer and some at four feet for the winter. Of course I put something there also inside the fence to stop the rabbits from going out. Everything was finally ready to receive the rabbits and the dogs and I invited everybody in for a good snack that was appreciated by every one.

Danielle was ready to deliver our baby any time now. She was already on maternity leave for the last month and that was what hold me back for my trip to Alberta, because I wanted to be with her for the birth of our child. I wish I could have taken a paternity leave too, but I couldn't afford it time wise. Then Samuel came to this world crying like most babies who no doubt was just fine inside her mother. I sure can understand that.

It was a real great day for all three of us, but I couldn't help thinking that we should have our babies at the retirement time when we have all the time in the world to take care of the mother and the baby. Even though I'm a busy man I spent every moment that I could with Danielle and Janene did just that too. Danielle was well surrounded, but I wish I could have done a lot more. Janene's delivery was not that far away either and luckily Danielle will have time to get back on her feet to assist her when the time comes.

It was now time to go get the rabbits that we need in Alberta and that too was quite a challenge. I didn't worry too much about the way to catch them, but rather about the way to bring them back home alive and healthy. I anticipated too, seeing my friend, the dog's breeder with the intention to get a few of his dogs. I was glad that the trip was a success. I only lost one rabbit out of thirty. The harvest was rather good. I heard one day that there were more rabbit in Calgary than people and this is a town of around eight hundred thousand people. I took the plane to go and I came back with a rented moving truck. I bought the thirty cages in Calgary and everything else that I needed to bring them home safely. I also brought back six little Mutesheps puppies from different parents and a couple of adults. I already knew that they were sled dogs. If my children like dogs like I do they will have a happy childhood. I never forgot the fun I had with them when I was a kid. In fact if it wasn't for the dogs I had, I simply wouldn't have had a childhood, because my father was putting me to work constantly. I still wonder why when my father was playing the fiddle we had to put our dog outside, because he wouldn't stop howling. I had a few years back, a female dog, my passed away little Princess who laid down on my foot and let herself be rock to the sound of my fiddle. It's certainly not because I play better than my dad, because I don't, I call my dad the fiddler with the magic bow.

One day when I was walking my new property, the one on the East side I discovered something quite special.

There was it seems like thousands of little trees that seem not to have enough space to grow properly. It is then that I got the idea to rescue them all from the ground and to replant them in a straight line and at a proper space on the East farm. It became a very nice plantation. We now have some pine, some spruce, some fir, some birch, which will be very good for our firewood, beside hockey sticks, some cedar, and also a nice row of maple trees. I also planted a good number of apple trees behind our house. I just love the McIntosh. No need to tell you that I will keep an eye on the little ones and make sure to make them fruitful.

We did not to bad with the dear as well. I got two bucks, three does and two fawns. It was worth our troubles. I was thinking also about making the rabbit field bigger just to make sure they have enough food. It was then that I decided to plant a large quantity of clover which I thought would save a lot of trees. My young apprentice carpenter became a very good agriculturist and there is no way I could change his mind now. He is now my handyman and that is why when he suggested staying on our property I didn't hesitate one bit. I told him; "Michel Larivière, if you're very serious you will help me at no cost to me for labour and we will build you a cottage by the river. It cannot be to close to the beach though, because I still would like my privacy when I'm swimming with my two women. In fact I plan to build one for us also near the beach. He agreed and he promised me complete discretion.

Then came the time to recruit the seamstresses that we need to put our articles together and the workers for the slaughterhouse. I was looking for a tanning expert, a good cook, an expert in canning, a publicist and a commercial traveler who would be busy finding business promises all across Canada. After many discussions with my partners I came to the conclusion that the best formula would be cookies for dogs that would be very nutritious and canned food for cats. Both can be a long time on shelves and still be good. That is very important especially when you start, because it's not known and it might not sell for a long time even if it's the best food in the world. On the containers it will be posted; "This food is especially made for dogs and cats, but is not improper for human consumption. Warning, it could cause cancer.

My wives thought that this could scare most people away from buying our product, but I agued differently. The same warning is on cigarette parks for many years and people continue to smoke anyway, besides, cancer is always rising. When you're stock, you're stock. They admitted that I might just be right and besides, this way our company, Rabbitech, is protected.

"By the way girls, I caught on the news that there were a lot less cancer cases in India than there were in North America. I just wondered if they eat less pork, less vermin than we do." "I mainly worry about those dogs and cats that you might make sick." "And I worry about the world population that I think is dying with a little deadly bite at the time. I think cancer is a little bug inside us that is feeding on what ever it needs to grow. For example the lungs cancer is feeding on smoke and keeps growing for as long as people are smoking. I knew a man who only had six months to live according to his doctor, but added seven years to his life by quitting smoking. The worst in all this is that children inherit the disease from their parents. This is not really the king of inheritance I want to leave to my children. If all the smokers knew that not only they are killing themselves when they smoke, but they're also killing their offspring maybe a lot of them would quit. Researchers are spending billions of dollars for a cure of that lazy disease and I believe that the answer is in the bible. I guess they have look everywhere but there."

We also needed about one thousand pigs to make sure we had a balanced nutritious food from both meat and that is why I made a large portion of the East farm a pasture for them. Pigs were going to cultivate and enrich the soil for us at the same time. This is why I planted fruits and vegetables in great quantity and get them delivered directly to the poor people who needed them. Everything grows quite good with pigs shit as a fertilizer.

We cannot if we are God's children get the money by millions of dollars and ignore the poor at the same time. I knew very well that I needed to have a good bunch of it save for the day that I will be attacked either by the government or the church. It was not only important for me to give food to the poor, but also to supply them with what ever it takes for them to start their own gardening. In one of my trip I showed them how to witch for water. The ground is like a human body, it's full of veins and when you pierce one it gives you what ever it holds. There is water almost everywhere, but you need to know how to find it. I looked around to find someone who could learn from me, someone with this gift. Let me tell you that they were in demand after that and became quite rich for their region. Where ever I went there is water now even in some place I was told I would never find any. Generally we can find water in less than twenty feet deep. Nevertheless I got those gift people to promise me to never abuse their new power if they want to keep it forever. Is there a need to tell you that in a lot of these places now a lot of them think I'm God. I got to tell you too that where I went the word of Jesus is also seeded. I put a lot of efforts to explain them the difference between God and a person who walks with God.

Chapter 6

Talking about money I would have needed a lot just to register my inventions and that is why I got the idea to post a little ad in the papers and on the internet that goes like this: Men who owns many important inventions seeks financial help from honest and serious people interested in sharing the profit at fifty per cent. If interested join me at James Prince..... It didn't take very long that I had over twenty answers, but the most interesting came by Email. Many of them asked me to tell them what I had over the phone and on the internet. Come on people, get serious would you?

Danielle would you come to see this please?" "What is it?" "Look for yourself. "I am very interested in your ideas. Please don't make any deals before I have a chance to see what you have. If still available I will take a plane tonight and be there tomorrow by noon. I'm waiting for an answer, Laurent."

"Could that be the same man?" "That would explain why he's so much in a hurry all the time. He travels the whole world looking for other people ideas and getting rich with them at the same time." "You have nothing to lose by listening to what he has to offer. We got a real good deal the last time we answered him." "I'm afraid he wouldn't give me much time to think things over." "Then think about it before you meet him, that's all." "You're right and it's all considered, I'll meet him and see what he's got to offer." "So don't waste any time and answer him."

"Hi Laurent. I am interested to meet you before any one else if you are very serious and if I can trust you with this, James."

"If he is just as quick with this as he was with your condo, I wouldn't have to wait too long. There is already an answer, let's see what it is. "Give me the name and address of your bank and your full name with your birth date and I'll sent you ten thousands dollars to the desk for you. If I meet my appointment with you that money will go towards our agreement if not the money will be yours with no question asked. Answer me if you agree and if not forget about me, Laurent." "Agreed, meet me tomorrow at noon at the Grandma restaurant in Trois-Rivières Quebec. Here is my name and……James."

Laurent met me at the said time the next day.

"Good day M Charron." "How do you know my name? I don't remember giving you my last name." "You gave it to me two years ago." "I don't remember you and yet I think I got a good memory."

I quickly understood that he was getting nervous probably thinking that he was trapped. His bodyguard also straightened up all of the sudden.

"Don't you worry, I met you two years ago when you bought my wives' condominium." "Ho yea, it was you who took the decision for one of them, now I remember you. The least I can say is that you can take a quick decision." "Some decisions are easy to make." "I brought some non discloser forms which are essential in this kind of transactions and when they are signed by you and me I will ask you to tell me one of your ideas. That would be enough for me to make you an offer." "Your bodyguard there, is not deaf, is he?" "I don't think I have anything to fear from you. Go Jos, go wait for me in the car, would you?"

It was obvious that he wasn't only a chauffeur. There was no doubt in my mind that he was also a bodyguard.

"You already know that I have a dozen of these inventions, don't you?" "What do you mean a dozen, is that ten, eleven, twelve or thirteen?" "I have thirteen of them." "Then describe one of them to me, not the best one and not the least either, would you?" "Then I'll pick this one here." "And you say that you have better than this?" "Yes sir!" "Then I'm giving you ten millions for all of them." "You kidding me sir, just one of them is worth more than ten times this amount." "I know but the cost of registering the patent and cost of the marketing is also millions of dollars." "I know all of this sir and this is why I called for someone like you." "How much do you want then?" "I don't want anything sir, I mean, I don't want money." "You do want something for all of this." "I want a fifty-fifty association sir." "Sixty forty!" "No, fifty-fifty!" "Sixty forty and that is my last offer." "Sixty forty is alright if you take the forty per cent sir." "You're not too easy to negotiate with, but I like your style, you've got a head on your shoulders. Fifty-fifty is alright for me too. Would you show me another one of your inventions?" "I will the day that this one here is on the way to success." "You're not easy, but like I said I like your style. I was just like you when I started. For what I saw, we're not done doing business together just yet." "What about the ten thousands that you sent me?" "It should rightfully come back to me, but keep it as a proof of good faith from my part. You're going to hear about it soon, because with me things don't drag too long and I have what it takes to get things moving. And you are right, what you just showed me will figure out about the one hundred millions." "I thank you very much, because I appreciate honesty. Good, I wouldn't retain you any longer. I know that by nature you're not wasting your time. Just one more little thing I want to tell you before you go and that is about the man who forced your door just after you bought the condo. He has totally changed since." "What is he doing now?" "He's spreading the word of God mainly to the prisoners and you couldn't pay him enough to do something wrong anymore." "That means he will succeed. If you see him just tell him that I have forgiven him." "I'll take care of the restaurant's bill." "It's already taken care of. Did you see anybody come in since we're here?" "No and it is rather strange at diner time, isn't it?" "I don't let any one disturb me when I discuss business." "I see, I'll try to always remember this. See you soon. It was a pleasure to discuss with you." "For me too and I'll give you some news very soon James. Bye for now!"

It's not always easy to hide our emotions, but I felt a huge need to scream out with the whole strength of my lungs and that is exactly what I did as soon as I turned the little road that lead to our property. I stopped my vehicle then I stepped outside of it and I screamed as loud as I could for about five minutes. When I got home I didn't have anymore voice. Danielle tried to get something out of me, but I couldn't push out a single word. I took my pen and I wrote on a piece of paper, fifty millions dollars.

"Don't give me that shit James, you're not funny at all."

I pointed out to her the piece of paper that I just gave her.

"This is not something to joke about James I will not lose my voice over this I will lose my whole head."

Then I wrote again.

"No point losing your head, it's only money." "Just a minute I will put a warm sock around your throat. What did you do to lose your voice like this? Come to lay down, you can talk later."

A half an hour later my voice started to come back and I asked her if she had something to calm me down.

"What are you going to do with all this money?" "I will certainly spend the first million getting a letter circulating around the world and if that is not enough then I'll spend the second one too. You know there are so many things that we can do with this money and that's not all, this is only for the one invention." "And how many do you have now?" "I have another twelve and this one I'm sure is not the best one." "You are a real genius." "It's not me who is a genius darling, it's God. He's the One who gave me all those ideas." "Nobody will believe you." "But you believe me, don't you?" "Of course I believe you, you only tell the truth." "Then others will believe me too. I will write our story if you allow me to and publish it, surely someone will believe the power of God. They wouldn't be able to do otherwise when they see what God have done for me and my family." "You want to write our story, do you really think that it could interest a lot of people?" "But sweetie there is a lot of men who are dreaming to have more than one wife, but to do so they have to divorce and remarry. Many have to do it many times. It ends up costing a lot of money. Some men go as far as killing their wives thinking to be free that way. But I have to admit that it's not easy to find two women that are not the least jealous. I know that for me it would have been impossible to be in our relationship if one of you would have been jealous." "What would you have done if one of us was?" "I don't want to think about it, but certainly it would have been very difficult. I would have had to pick the one who wasn't jealous or forget about both of you. It would have been very hard, almost impossible I think." "You said that you want to make a letter circulate around the world?" "Yes, I wrote it a little while ago and it's now time that the whole world take notice of it. That's what God is asking me to do and I must obey Him. That will infuriate the beast, but I don't care, I'll do it anyway." "You're going to get killed." "I'm going to write anonymously, this way it's not going to be easy for anyone to find me. Maybe this is why the money seems to come from heaven, some of it will be use to defend myself and even to hide if necessary. I might even have to change my name one day, who knows? Here is that letter. Do you want to read it?

This letter is from a Jesus' disciple to the entire world.

If you knew

It is not easy to decide where to begin, for there are so many lies and contradictions in the bible, for the ones who want to see them of course. I will do my very best to expose a few that are susceptible to touch you or to open your eyes, something that Jesus really like to do. He said in Matthew 13, 25;" "But while everyone was sleeping, his enemy (and he said that it was the devil) came and sowed the lies among the truth." "The truth that he himself was seeding.

They are there those lies and I am sure that you will see them too, if only you make an effort to look. No matter what I say, but him, Jesus, listen to him as God Himself asked you to do. See Matthew 17, 5.

There are some big lies and some of them are very obvious. Take for example John 3, 16, it is written;" "For God so loved the world." "But God asked his disciples to withdraw from the world, not to live in the world. He basically said that the world is the way to hell. I personally know that the world is the kingdom of the devil and you have the proof in Matthew 4, 8.

It is said in the same verse John 3, 16 that God gave his one and only son, which means that Jesus was his first born. It is said in Luke 3, 38 that Adam is also the son of God. It is written that Jesus is the only son, and not me, but the bible proves otherwise. That is a lot in only one verse, but there is more.

Now it is written in Genesis 6, 1- 2;

"When men began to increase in number on the earth, and daughters were born to them, the sons of God saw that the daughters of men were beautiful, and they married any of them they choose." "So according to this, there were more sons of God. Take a look also in Deuteronomy 32, 19." "The Lord saw this and rejected them because He was angered by his sons and daughters."

"So according to these words from the bible, it is not true that Jesus is God's only son.

In fact I think I am the son of God too because I do his will.

According to the Christian believes I am God's brother, because they say that Jesus is God became man, and the same Jesus said that the one who does the will of his Father in heaven is his brother, his sister and his mother. Look Matthew 12, 50.

But let's go back to John 3, 16. According to this, God sacrificed is first born, because it is said that he is the only one. Go read 2 Kings 16, 3;" "He walked in the ways of Israel and even sacrificed his son in the fire following the detestable ways of the nations the Lord had driven out before the Israelites." "God would have chased some nations in front of the nation of Israel because they were offering their sons in sacrifice and He would have done the same thing??????????, Please. For what? To save the children of the devil, the sinners. Look in 1 John 3, 6 -10.

I will tell you what is the truth and you can reed it in Deuteronomy 18, 18;" "I will raise up from them a prophet like you (Moses) from among their brothers, I will put my words in his mouth, and he will tell them everything I command him." "That is what Jesus was sent for, to preach to us, to tell us what to do to be save, and what Jesus told us? Look in Matthew 4, 17. "Repent for the kingdom of heaven is near." That is the truth either you want to believe it or not. Turn to God, not to anyone else. When did you hear Jesus say pray Marie or Joseph or any mortal? He didn't even say to pray Jesus, but he said to pray the Father in heaven. See Matthew 6, 9 – 14. When you pray anyone else, you pray the dead and it is an insult to God. It is impossible to men to live without sin, but with God everything is possible.

When Jesus said to the adulteress, I don't condemn you, he also said something else very important and that was; "Go now and sin no more." He wouldn't have said that if it was impossible.

"That is the way to be saved and if you do sin, God will forgive you as long as you truly repent. See John 8, 11 and 5, 14.

There is a very important message in Matthew 24, 15." "So when you see in the holy place (the holy bible) the abomination that causes desolation, may the reader be careful when he reads." "That is what I ask you to do, not only to be careful of what you read, but to be careful to whom you talk to, because the beast is still killing the disciples of Jesus.

There is another abomination that I would like to talk to you about. You can find it in Mathew 1, 18." "She was found to be with child through the Holy Spirit." "Was that the same Holy Spirit that was not yet in the world? According to John 14, 26, 15, 26 and 16, 7 Jesus was to send the Holy Spirit down as soon as he was going to be with his Father in heaven. When we know that God was so mad when the angels took the pretty girls in the time of Noah, that He almost destroyed the whole earth and all the people on it, and He would have done the same thing to get Marie, mother of Jesus pregnant. It is simply a total none sense. Look again at Genesis 6, 1- 2. If I understand well here, the sons of God, (The spirits or angels if you like it better) had sexual desires. It is possible to talk about these things today, because the knowledge has increased. See Daniel 12, 4;" "Many will go here and there to increase knowledge." "That is what I'm doing. We don't need to be a genius or a scientist to know now days and to witness this phenomenal truth. It is true that there are some things that are hard to understand, but, there are others that are very simple and easy.

Take for example the Paul's rapture. See 1 Thessalonians 4, 16 -17.

"For the Lord himself will come down from heaven, with a loud command, with the voice of the archangel and with the trumpet call of God, and the dead in Christ will rise first. After that, we who are still alive and are left will be caught up together with them in the clouds to meet the Lord in the air. And so we will be with the Lord forever."

"There he is, the bird will be caught in the air. For one thing, we are not dead in Christ, but we are alive. It is though up to you to be caught in the air with him and his followers.

Let me tell you what Jesus said now. See Matthew 13, 41– 43;" "The son of men (means prophet) will send out his angels, and they will weed out of his Kingdom (means on earth) everything that causes sin and all who do evil. They will throw them into the fiery furnace, where there will be weeping and gnashing of teeth. Then the righteous will shine like the sun in the kingdom of their Father. He, who has ears, let him hear." Do you want to shine like the sun in the kingdom of God with me or be caught up in the air and be thrown in the fiery furnace?

It was said that Jesus died for our sins. Personally I think that if someone who would give his life for our sins it would have to be the devil, he likes them. When it comes to Jesus, he said that if we follow him (the word of God) we would never die, that we will have eternal life. That also means that he is still alive. He told us also what he would do with the one who keeps sinning. See Matthew 7, 23;" "Then I will tell them plainly, I never knew you. Away from me you evildoers!" "(sinners) Jesus repeats the same message when he talks about the judgment of the nations. Mathew 25, 31- 46. That's what he said also in the explanation of the parable of the weeds. Do you still feel like saying, that we all have sins? Matthew 13, 41.

I will end with two different messages, one from Jesus and the other one from Paul.

Jesus told us in Matthew 5, 17 – 18; "Do not think that I have come to abolish the Law or the prophets, I have not come to abolish them but to fulfill them, I tell you the truth, until heaven and earth disappear, not the smallest letter, not the least stroke of a pen, will by any means disappear from the Law."

"God said, Jeremiah 31, 36. "Only if these decrees vanish from my sight declares the Lord will the descendants of Israel ever cease to be a nation before me." Now I don't know if you are blind enough not to see the earth and heaven or yet not to see that the nation of Israel still exist, but the truth is that they're still all there.

On the other hand there is Paul who said that the Law is gone, disappeared. See Galatians 3, 25 ; "We are no longer under the supervision of the Law." See also Ephesians 2, 15; "By abolishing in his flesh the Law with its commandments and regulations."

"There is another one that I call a terrible if not the worst abomination in the bible. We all know that the goal of the devil is to condemn everybody. Go read Paul in Hebrews 6, 4 ; "It is impossible for those who have once been enlightened, (like the apostles) who have tasted the heavenly gift, (like the Jesus' apostles) who have shared in the Holy Spirit (like the apostles) who have tasted the goodness of the word of God and the power of the coming age, (like the apostles) If they fall away, (like the apostles) to be brought back to repentance, because, to their lost they are crucifying the son of God all over again." Now if it is impossible for the Jesus' disciples to be saved, no one can be, but here what Jesus said to his apostles. Matthew 19, 27; "Jesus said to them, I tell you the truth, at the renewal of all things, when the son of man sits on his glorious throne, you who have followed me will also sit on twelve thrones, judging the twelve tribes of Israel." "Check it out yourself Jesus Matthew 5, 17 -18. "Do not think that I have come to abolish the Law or the prophets, I have not come to abolish them but to fulfill them, I tell you the truth, until heaven and earth disappear, not the smallest letter, not the least stroke of a pen, will by any means disappear from the Law."

Now, can you compare that to Paul in Romans 10, 4 ? "Christ is the end of the Law, so that there may be righteousness for everyone who believes." There is a liar, but that is not Jesus.

Here is a bit of homework for you
Jesus Mat. 11, 19 versus Paul Gal. 2, 16
Jesus Mat. 10, 42
Jesus Mat. 16, 27
James. 2, 14 – 24
And many more

I'm going to let you digest all this, because I know that it is not going to be easy for everybody. On the other hand, if you want to get some more, just know that I got another five hundred and more.

Remember that I worn you to be careful of who you talk to. Louis Riel confided in his so called friends, a bishop and in many priests and he died young, but not before being locked up for three years in St Jean de Dieu, an asylum in East Montreal on a pretext to protect and hide him from persecution. They accused him of treason against the state, but in reality it was against the Catholic Church, but it was not the church of Jesus Christ. The church of Jesus would not have him killed or condemned him to death. If you talk to someone who have a business like a church to protect or to defend don't expect to be welcome, neither you nor the word of God. Jesus too worn us see Matthew 10, 16; "I am sending you out like sheep among wolves." It is serious, be careful. Remember though that the work for God is never lost.

The last time I had a message from God; it was in a dream as most of the time. The message was to let you know my knowledge about these things.

The dream

I was crying and I told God that there was no point to tell anyone about all this, because nobody, but nobody listen to what I have to say and everybody argues the truth. He told me then ; " You don't have to worry about this at all, all I ask you is to tell them either they listen or not or what they think or say, this way no one will be able to blame me. They will know that I sent them someone to wake them up." "That was the end of the dream! It was for me the most peaceful message I have ever received from Him, but it was also a message that told me to do it. If you're ever afraid to lose your mind or anyone accuses you of that, you can answer this, it is better to lose an eye or a hand than to lose the whole body, see Matthew 5, 29 - 30. I would like to add to this; It is better to lose you're mind than to lose your soul.

My Goal is to get this letter circulating around the world and that in all possible languages. That is also the goal of Jesus and God.

See Mathew 28, 19-20; "Therefore go and make disciples of all nations, and teaching them to obey everything I have commanded you, and surely I am with you always, to the very end of the age."

"Now if you want to be part of Jesus' gang, you can make as many copies as you can and send them to as many people as you can. It is possible also to do everything you can to stop it and to get me executed. The decision is totally yours and so will be your judgment in front of Jesus (the word of God).

Good luck! James." Jesus said he is with us and truly the word of God is still with us.

"But darling this letter is out of this world, it looks like it was written by an ancient time prophet." "I'm only a Jesus' disciple sweetie and nothing more. It seems at times that we're the only ones in the world so much that everybody is surprised to hear that disciples exist still today, someone who really knows the word of God. Don't you think this is terrible?" "What you're saying is true, even my parents seem to be stunned by your teaching and they're not school kids. Everyone whom I know and who went to talk to their priest or their pastor could see that it was bothering them when they heard about these things. The pastor of the church where I was going in Westside BC strictly warned his congregation to not come near me or talk to me.

The word of God, the real truth is very dangerous for the churches anyway and it could be contagious as well. It is a very good Baptist Evangelical church. Why do you think that the scribes and the Pharisees were looking everywhere for Jesus and tried to kill him? They also accused him of breaking the law by healing someone on a Sabbath day. They said that he had a demon and more yet, they accused him of being the devil. Look in Matthew 10, 25. "If they have called the master of the house Beelzebub, how much more will they call his disciples?" That is what church's people do. We have to know that in those days they would cut off the head of someone who was caught picking up a piece of wood on Saturday especially if he didn't have any money to pay the fine. Jesus said that he (the devil) was a murderer from the beginning. A few years back I made a small garden where I planted some potatoes, but I was too busy to take care of it for the rest of the summer. When I went back to see what happened at the time of the harvesting I only found a few potatoes, because the weeds had completely invaded the garden. They were up to four and a half feet tall. The same way the potatoes weren't easy to find among the weeds, the truth is not easy to find among the lies. Although Jesus said that both of them (the truth and the lies) will be together until the end time. Look at Matthew 13, 39-40. If the beast could have got rid of the truth completely it would have done it by now, but luckily for us the beast had to use the word of God as well to attract a clientele. Unfortunately it is true too that there are a lot of lies and not that much of truth. The truth is that the truth was hidden by the weeds (the lies) just as Jesus said it two thousand years ago. I got the undisputable proof that we are at the end time, because the harvesting has started. The truth is coming out and the beast will not be happy at all about it. If you read up till now you probably already understand who is this beast that Jesus talked to us about. Just in case that you are scared, just remember that the end time of this devilish world will be the beginning of the one thousand years of the word of God reign. Jesus is the word of God so it's the word of God that will reign for one thousand years. I can't wait for this to happen. That reign should be easy because the devil will be tied up for one thousand years and all the sinners will be locked up as well just like Jesus said it in Matthew 13, 39-43. Think about it for two seconds, nobody to hurt us anymore that in itself would be hell for the demons and heaven for us. That would make them gnashing their teeth. God created the world in six days (six thousand years) and He rested on the seventh day (one thousand years. Look at 2 Peter 3, 8 it is clear to me that God couldn't rest for as long as the devil is roving around the earth and deceiving billions of people. According to all the prophets, men is on earth for as long as six thousand years and God largely deserve his rest. All the nations are on the verge to find out about the truth and I'm very glad to be part of this gigantic challenge. I got to say that I asked God to use me the way He sees me fit for it. I'm happy for the trust He puts in me.

"But when will He come Darling?" "According to what Jesus said, only God the Father knows the day and the hour. Jesus himself doesn't know and it's just as well otherwise men would have tortured him trying to find out. This is why he asked us to stay on guard days and nights and be ready all the time. I know I am." "I am too." "I know you are and that is why I told you at our marriage that we'll be together for the eternity. You see this is the kingdom of heaven that Jesus talked about. We can read about it only in Matthew. This is why I doubt very much that the writers of the other three gospels ever saw or met Jesus." "The greatest thing that you ever did for me is to show me the truth." "This is the greatest thing you ever told me, my love. I love you almost as much as the word of God." "That means that you love me extremely and I know it. Jesus is the word of God and when he said that who ever loves is mother or father or anyone more than he (The word of God) is not worthy of the word of God. That was wrongly interpreted. It's the same thing when it comes to the little children when he said let the little children come to me, which means let the little children come to the word of God." "That was never presented to me this way. James you are a real prophet." "Danielle I told you before, I'm only a Jesus' disciple.

There is a lot of thing that were wrongly interpreted and the next one that I talk about is in Matthew 8, 21-22. "One of Jesus' disciples asked Jesus to let him go bury his dad first and Jesus told him to let the dead bury the dead, you follow me."

"How the dead can bury the dead? They certainly cannot come out of their coffin." "What if it meant; let the sinners bury the cadavers?" "Hey, this is powerful and it sure makes sense." "There is a more powerful message in those words, can you tell me what it is?" "This is a lot as it is, I don't see anything else." "Jesus just said about this disciple that he was sinless." "That's true too." "There is another one, do you see it?" "Come on, I'm not that blind after all, but I have to admit, I don't see anything else." "Alright then, let me heal you if you allow me to, which means to open your eyes on the subject. Jesus just told this disciple to follow him as well, what is that means?" "That's right too, you're right again, it means that Jesus needed him, a sinless disciple, and that he was in a hurry to the point of not let the disciple take the time to bury his dad." "Bravo! I don't want you to think that I want to make you look stupid, but there is another one in there." "Ho, come on, stop it." "I'm serious." "What is it?" "Jesus is telling us that we cannot do anything anymore for the people who passed away, so everyone who prays for the dead is wasting his time and is also annoying God." "Anyone who cannot see and believe that you were enlightened would have to be an incurable blind." "There will be a lot of them unfortunately. You see this is why I rarely go to funerals. It depresses me to see so many people praying for the dead. Kind David lamented for as long as his son was dying, but as soon as his son died he started celebrating. See 2 Samuel 12, 15-24. King David knew God and his word." "James, when I think about if I didn't meet you I would probably have never found out about the truth and it gives me shivers. God loves me." "God loves and blesses you mainly because you love Him and you are always ready to receive his word and turn around and make it known to others. That is what is called the good seed that fell in good soil. This is what is called; the light that shines in the darkness. When you receive and accept the word of God, you receive Jesus in your life and that is something that pleases God.

Well all this is good, but we also have to talk business if we want to keep feeding the poor in the world. I cannot see to everything and keep making you both happy. I got to find a supervisor, someone honest who can manage and is good delegating. Do you know anyone who could do that job?" "No I don't, but I think you do." "I don't see, who you have in mind?" "You have nothing but good to say about Bernard Sinclair." "I will have to talk to him, but first I need to talk to Janene about it, because for nothing in the world I would want her to be unease concerning him. For sure I don't want her to get her nails out again against him. When I think that his brother had nothing to do with his behaviour, I still blame myself for that." "We have to learn to forgive even ourselves." "You're right sweetie. I will talk to Janene tonight and if it's alright with her I'll talk to Bernard the sooner the better. I'm pretty sure that he needs a good job with a good salary."

"Bernard how are you doing my friend? Tell me what are you doing for work these days?" "Ho I work here and there, what ever I can get. It's not that easy to find a job when you just out of jail." "Tell me are you bilingual?" "Not at one hundred per cent, but I can help myself quite well. But James, why are you asking me all of these questions?" "I'm looking for a man on whom I can count to ease my duties. I got too much to look after." "Not that it matters much, but what would I have to do if you don't mind me asking?" "You would have to travel across the country and give assistance to some of my employees in some locations where things are not going too well. First tell me if you are interested or not and if you think you can do it." "I think I can do it, but it also depends on the salary that comes with it." "The salary will be good, trust me on that, but are you interested?" "Of course I am, keep talking." "Would you be interested in taking flying courses to become a pilot?" "That yes, I already have two years to my credit. I quit because I couldn't afford it anymore, but that was always my dream to become a pilot." "Don't tell me that you wanted to fly from the sixth floor?" "Don't tell me that you're going to come back on that, I thought it was far behind us?" "No, the only reason I talk about it is not to blame you or anything like that, but to worn you that I don't want Janene to feel angry at you ever again. She has forgiven you, but she didn't forget and me neither." "Neither one of you have anything to fear from me." "I believe you otherwise I wouldn't be here." "When can you start? What kind of salary am I getting?" "Would two hundred thousands dollars a year be enough for you?" "Dammit James, don't mock me please?" "What, this is not enough?" "I don't believe it." "If you can do the job I'm offering you and do it well, it's not going to be too much." "You're serious, two hundred thousands?" "You should know me enough to know that I never joke when I do business." "Tell me what to do and I'll start tomorrow, no right away boss." "Do you have a suit and a few clean shirts?" "I'm not dressed very well and I don't have much money either." "Nevermind dresses I want a man who wears pants." "You said you weren't joking in business." "Business is over, now it's time to talk about the pleasures in life. I'm giving you five thousands dollars to go buy clothes that you need to do the work." "You would do that?" "No, I'm doing it, here is the cheque. You always have to look like a real gentleman. I want you to represent me everywhere you work for me. You'll have to have an iron hand in a soft glove. Did you hear about the new sowing shop on Chemin des sables?" "Do you mean the rabbit skin shop? Everybody is talking about it." "It's mine so be there at nine o'clock tomorrow morning and stay there until I get there even if it's five o'clock in the afternoon." "I'll be there, see you tomorrow boss." "I prefer that you call me James." "Alright James, as you wish."

The next day I went to meet with Bernard at four thirty in the afternoon. I had arranged everything with the forewoman to show him the site and everything we were doing with the rabbit skin. I knew very well that the whole process should have taken only a couple of hours, but this man had to go through his first test. If he couldn't obey an order from one day to the next, he was not the man I needed for this job.

"Hi Bernard!" "Hi James, is everything alright? I was just wondering if I should wait any longer." "You did the right thing by waiting, because your new position was at stake. I like your suit, it fits you nicely." "But I didn't do anything all day." "You've met with our staff and you've learn about our products." "Yes, but that only took a couple of hours. I'm not the kind of guy who likes to get paid for doing nothing, you know." "Well, I'm glad to hear that, because you'll have a lot to do. I'm paying you eight hundred dollars today because I wanted to be sure that you can follow an order even if it's not pleasant. Now I want you to learn from my ways, because you'll have to do the same thing with a lot of my employees who need to be tested. The best way to find out if a man will be true to you is to talk with him about women, because if he can cheat on his wife who is supposed to be his number one in life don't expect him to be faithful to you. This individual is cheating on himself. If he can steal a nickel from you, he can also steal five thousands and more. Tomorrow you'll have another easy thing to do." "What would that be?" "I want you to go register yourself to finish your pilot course." "It should be no problem especially if I have the money to pay for it. The courses are very expensive, do you know?" "I want all the details, the days you'll be taking the courses, the time and the price, I pay for everything. I want to know how long it will normally take you." "I need to know what I will have to fly and if I'll need to fly outside of Canada." "That will be a fifty passengers company jet and you will have to fly everywhere in the world. I must be able to count on you at anytime. I will build you a house on one of my farm near the landing strip." "All this is very intriguing and knowing you I know that you don't do anything illegal. I have to admit though that I still have a problem believing in all of this." "Count all the cities in Canada that hold more than fifty thousand people and those are the places that you will have to land for now. Until you get your pilot license you will have to fly quite often with commercial companies. I hope you're not afraid to fly." "Very funny!"

"You are allowed to talk about the word of God to anyone who wants to hear it, but not on your working hours and you should never impose yourself. You will never work for me on the Sabbath day (Saturday) unless it is absolutely necessary and I don't talk about money here. That goes for all of my employees too and everywhere. You already know that God's blessing come with the obedience in his laws and his statutes." "Yes I know, but I forgot where it is written. Just give me a minute here that I remember, it's in Genesis 26, 4-5. "I will make your descendents multiply like the stars of heaven, and I will give all these countries to your posterity and all the nations of the world will be blessed through your posterity, because that Abraham obeyed my voice and kept my charge, my commandments, my statutes and my laws." This is a nice promise Bernard. I can tell you one thing and that is I cannot count all of my blessings anymore. God gave me a bunch of books that I wrote until now, hundred of songs, inventions, beautiful music, a wonderful family, I cannot count all my enterprises, and also the opportunity to feed thousands of people around the world. I cannot forget also the opportunity to spiritually heal people. I'm also predicting having more than one hundred thousand employees in the world within five years. God gave me the opportunity to become the richest man in the world, me a man who never looked for wealth. In the last three years nine of my enemies died and I wished no harm to any of them. Any point telling you that I find that a bit odd?" "I got to agree with you, it is strange." "It's just as if God wanted to show me that I shouldn't fear anyone, that my enemies will fall before me." "Don't look anywhere else that is surely the reason." "I wanted to ask you if you heard from your brother." "Not much, he doesn't write very often, but as far as I could understand he's not very happy." "I would like you to send him a letter that I wrote lately, one which I hope will go around the world." "Just a minute now, are you talking about the disciple's letter to the whole world? You're the one who wrote this letter? I received it and I sent it to at least one hundred people." "Did you send it to your brother?" "No, I'm sorry, but he never wanted to talk about those things." "You have to send him this letter even if all it does is giving you a piece of mind. He can always do what ever he wants with it." "You're right. I'll sent it to him tomorrow." "Why not today? By the same occasion could you ask him if he would be interested in a job in the underdeveloped countries, but without mentioning me, would you?" "Can you tell me what you have in mind?" "I'll tell you later if you don't mind. You can tell him that the salary will be good, but it will be a very hard work in a very difficult environment." "You don't want me to tell him where the offer is coming from?" "You'll tell him later if you do now he wouldn't even have a chance to consider it, because it would be coming from me, one of his enemies from his point of view. I don't want to influence his decision. Let me know as soon as he asks more information. I'll leave you with this and keep me informed, would you? Here is a cell phone, it's yours for all is concerning your work, but you're not to abuse it, because just remember that a dollar saved in this country could save the life of one person in an undeveloped country." "I never thought of it that way." "See you soon."

In the mean time Laurent was working on my third invention and he was more and more excited about it. He told me that if this one was just as successful as the other two he would spend all his time working on the rest of my inventions. It's promising. Wood grows just like mushrooms, which means very fast on my farms because of one of my last inventions. There is a reason why in British Columbia in the Vancouver region wood grows almost all year round. It's because it doesn't freeze. We can sell our wood at a low price or yet use it in a more efficient way. I built a shop to make trim boards like casing and base boards and all. This way a twenty years old tree is worth more than two hundred dollars which is ten times more than for regular lumber. It's worth putting a warm sock on the tree foot for the winter.

In all of this I knew too that one day the beast would want to put a price on my head and this is why I also built a replica of our house on one of the Caribbean Islands. Right now it is rented out to a rich industrial company president for a reasonable price.

We have now four children who are of a docility model, a boy and a girl from each mother and it's not over yet. I had to adopt Janene's children to give them a legal status, this way everybody is happy. Any point to say that they've started asking a lot of questions?

Bernard has been flying a lot of hours and once a month he brings back his brother from Africa or from somewhere else. Raymond's duties are always where the needs are the most urgent. I showed him how to build some shacks with the insulated boards and in turn he shows these poor people how to do it. Those shacks are giving good shade in the summer and good shelters in the winter plus they are absolutely water proof.

The letter is still working its way around the world and the governments pressed by the churches are looking for the people who initiate it. There is a lot less people who give their money to those churches today and they have to sell their gold to pay their bills. When gold was worth thirty-nine dollars an ounce the chalice was worth sixty thousand dollars and the ciborium was worth one hundred thousand dollars in gold. Yet there are many Christian children and non Christian who walk bare feet everywhere in the world, because they are too poor to buy some shoes. Today gold is worth around one thousand dollars an ounce which is twenty-fife times more. That is a good enough reason for the churches to keep their solid door locked. The leaders of those churches will soon or later face the one who inspired me this letter, Jesus Christ, my master. This one man from God who said not to accumulate treasures on earth. See Matthew 6, 19-20. This is from James Prince, a Jesus' disciple who is hoping that you have appreciated those few commentaries. I wish you the best of luck and may God inspire you too. To be continued